BLOOD AND GOLD

Fresh blood soaked into the gunman's shirt as he pressed his left hand to his chest. "Damn! My firin' hand! You busted it all up!"

"I could've done worse. Was it worth it?" Spur asked.

Spit drooled from the wounded man's lips; his body trembled as pain boiled through him. "Hell, yeah, it's worth it! Anything's worth them dies!"

The word thundered through Spur's brain but he showed no surprise, no emotion at the mention of his secret cargo—the dies for the twenty-dollar gold piece. "It's just your hand. You may be crazy, lefty, but you're not dying. They'll get you patched up in jail."

Clutching his broken hand to his narrow chest, the downed man reached into his shirt with his good one. "I ain't dying, mister, you are!"

Spur #27

FRISCO FOXES

Dirk Fletcher

LEISURE BOOKS ∞ NEW YORK CITY

A LEISURE BOOK

Published by

Dorchester Publishing Co. Inc.
6 East 39th Street
New York, NY 10016

Printed in the United States of America

FRISCO FOXES

1

"You're dead, mister!"

Spur McCoy spun around, his firing hand sliding down to the holster strapped to his right thigh. He gripped his .45, swung it up and searched for the man who'd yelled at him.

The deserted Hastings, Arizona Territory street was shot through with inky shadows. Spur studied the darkened buildings and black alleys, looking for some sign of movement.

He let the saddle fall to the ground behind him and stood upright, knees slightly bent, gripping his Colt with a firm, steady hand.

Nothing. No sound, no voices. Spur sighed. He was just keyed up. The job had been easy, too easy. Maybe he was just expecting trouble.

Boots pounded in the dirt somewhere to the right, across the street near a false-front. The echoes seemed to emanate from the alley between Feingold's Dry Goods and the Thompson Hotel. He studied the wide passage but saw no movement, no greyish figure, no glint of moonlit steel in its blackness.

Raucous music mixed with liquor-charged voices blasted out from the saloon half a block down as the doors burst open. A drunken cowboy stumbled out, reeled and lurched back inside.

Silence settled around him again.

"Show yourself!" Spur barked.

The man snorted. "Hell, I ain't that stupid! Got you right where I want you. Now give 'em here!"

"Give you what? Make sense, asshole!"

Feet rustled in the alley again. Spur still couldn't see the man. He cursed. If he hadn't spent so much time playing poker in that smoky saloon he'd be snoring away in his cold hotel bed by now.

Guess I'll have to flush him out, Spur thought. He'd circle around the dry goods store and surprise the gunman from behind.

Soft kerosene light blossomed from the hotel's alley-facing windows as he began to move. Someone—perhaps that pretty blonde-haired serving girl—had lit the lamps. The glow illuminated a tall, wiry man leaning against the wall of the dry goods store.

The gunman peered at Spur, clumsily gripping a six-gun in his left hand. Surprised by the light and suffering from alcoholic confusion, the man stared wildly as he realized he'd lost the advantage.

"Damnation!" he drunkenly thundered.

"What in hell do you want?" Spur asked, sweetening his aim on the suddenly nervous man.

"You know what I want," he blurted. "It's what you've been carrying around for two weeks. And it's what you're gonna give me right now!"

"What, my poker winnings? You could've won 'em from me at the table. You're stinking drunk. Go crawl in a corner and sleep it off." McCoy approached him cautiously.

Did he know? And if so, *how*?

"The hell I will!" he said, smirking. "You just hold it right there, mister! Come any closer and I'll . . . I'll plug your heart full of lead!"

Spur laughed as he approached the man with

short, deliberate steps. "You got me shaking in my boots," he said sarcastically. "You're so drunk you couldn't hit your right ball, if you had one."

The left-handed man's face reddened at the insult. "No one talks to me like that, asshole!" he said. "No one! Now give 'em to me!"

"You really wanna die that bad? I'm tired of playing games. Back off and throw down your weapon." Spur's voice was harsh.

"Like hell!" The man's arm shook so violently he nearly dropped his revolver.

The man's features came into sharper view as Spur approached him. He was sweating, the veins on his head popping out. His closely-spaced eyes darted from side to side. The gunman's chest heaved with labored breath.

Gunman? Hell, Spur thought. This guy was scared to death. He'd probably never aimed at a man before.

"That's close enough. No more time," the wiry man said. He twisted up his face in anguish. "It's now or never! You've got my ticket to more money than I could ever make in this hell-hole and I'm gonna take it from you!"

His aim shifted up and down as if he couldn't see Spur clearly. His emaciated body shook with fear.

"Do it," Spur yelled. "Go ahead. Try to blast me into hell. Give me a good reason for splattering your worthless guts all over the goddamned street!" He stopped ten feet from the shivering man.

Rage surged through the left-hander. His finger squeezed. The revolver spat.

The shot slammed harmlessly into the dust five yards from McCoy's boots. Before the explosion finished echoing between the false-fronted buildings, Spur blasted a slug into the drunkard's left hand.

The hot metal ripped into the man's extremity, splintering bones, severing nerves and arteries on its path of destruction. Blood, looking dark brown in the thin light, spurted out of the wound as the gunman's weapon rattled to the dust-filled street.

The thin man went down, clutching his shattered hand. His face went white and a howl of rage-infused pain strangled out of his throat.

"Jesus H. Christ!" he screamed.

Spur moved closer, his long-barrelled Colt .45 trained on the laboring chest. "What the hell do you want? An executioner? Sorry, that costs extra."

He glanced at the saddle before swinging his head back to the man. Good; it was still there.

The left-hander's face distorted with pain. "You know damn well what I want," he spluttered. Fresh blood soaked into his shirt as he pressed his left paw to his chest. "Damn! My firin' hand! You busted it all up!"

"I could've done worse. Was it worth it, lefty?"

Spit drooled from his lips. The wounded man's body trembled as pain boiled through him. "Hell, yeah, it's worth it! Anything's worth them dies!"

The word thundered through Spur's brain but he showed no surprise, no emotion at the mention of his secret cargo. "What the hell're you talking about?"

Doors banged open. Yells rang through the sleepy town as residents hurried outside to watch the excitement.

The thin man howled. "Goddamn it hurts!"

"It's just your hand. You may be crazy, lefty, but you're not dying. They'll get you all patched up in jail."

Clutching his broken hand to his narrow chest,

the downed man reached into his shirt with his good one. "I ain't dying, mister, you are!"

Spur drove a bullet into the man's chest long before he had the opportunity to use the suddenly revealed derringer. The man's eyes grew wide with shock as the slug blasted an inch-wide hole through his heart.

The left-hander's body shook as his big pump exploded. His arms and legs jerked spastically for several seconds before going limp. A long, hissing breath passed out between the dead man's lips as his blank eyes centered on the thin moon hanging above his motionless form.

Seven men and a brave dance-hall girl crowded around Spur, craning their necks, whooping and talking.

"He dead, Smitty?" the young woman asked the man next to her.

"Course he's dead!"

The whore whistled. "Hell, I ain't never seen a dead man afore, only men dead between their legs."

"Shut your pretty little mouth, Angelique, and get back to work!" the burly man thundered.

Spur stepped back, away from the crowd, still looking at the recently departed.

"Now you just hold it right there, mister."

The voice, cracking with youth, seemed to be directed to him.

McCoy sighed. What now? He slowly turned around as the curious residents of Hastings, Arizona Territory continued to comment on the deceased.

A stocky young man, carrying a rifle, warily approached McCoy. He looked barely old enough to shave. "Mister, you're under arrest for killing Frank Johnson."

"Ah hell, Enos, leave him alone! It was self-defense, plain and simple," a grizzled man said. "Saw the whole thing. Wow, what a show!"

"Yeah, Enos, just like Dodge City!" another called.

The star pinned on the youth's chest told Spur all he needed to know.

"Is that true?" Enos asked him.

"Yeah."

The boy glanced at the dead man, then back up at Spur. His fresh face wrinkled with thought. "I'm the law around these parts," he said hesitantly. "At least, since this afternoon when the sheriff rode out with a posse to find the man who robbed Mrs. Ortega."

"Look, deputy, I'm gonna get my saddle. We'll talk about this in your office."

"I—I—"

Spur shot him a steel-eyed glance. The kid clamped shut his thin lips, smiled nervously, then nodded.

McCoy retrieved his saddle, flung it over his back and followed the greenhorn to the sheriff's office.

Once there, Spur explained as much as the kid needed to know. He didn't tell the sweating youth everything, just enough to put off any more questions.

"But—but why was Johnson tryin' to kill you?" Enos asked, scratching his sandy-haired scalp. "He wasn't good for nothing, but he never hurt nobody. Not as long as I've seen him around town."

"How in hell should I know?" Spur growled, glancing at his saddle. No sense in spreading the word around; too many people seemed to know.

"I don't understand—"

"Look, maybe he lost two dollars at the poker table. Maybe his missus wouldn't give it to him—"

"He don't—*didn't*—have a missus," Enos said, blushing.

"Maybe he just threw too much whiskey down his throat and had to prove he was a man."

"Maybe," the boy said thoughtfully. He rubbed his double-chin.

"I'm only passing through here, deputy. I don't have time for your local trouble. And I need my sleep if I'm gonna catch the ten o'clock stage in the morning." He hefted his saddle and started for the door. "You have any problem with that, boy?" McCoy curled his upper lip, arched his left eyebrow and dared him with his eyes.

Enos looked away and fumbled with a bag of fixings. "No. Heck, they all said it was self-defense." He shrugged and smiled blankly. "I guess it was."

Grunting, Spur hefted his saddle and slammed outside. He walked to his hotel with measured steps, went up the stairs, unlocked the door, shut it and pushed the key into the lock. Inside he threw the saddle onto the bed, kicked off his boots and flopped down on the hard mattress.

He rested his head on the saddle, smelling its rich, new-leather scent, and thought of the treasures it contained. They were so valuable that gunmen were willing to risk death to obtain them.

At six-foot, two-inches, two hundred pounds and thirty-two years of age, Spur McCoy was the top agent in the newly-formed Secret Service. After a distinguished career in the infantry during the Civil War, McCoy had joined the service as soon as it was created by Congress in 1858.

The reddish-brown hair that touched his shirt collar and rode along his upper lip was usually covered with a low-crowned, gray Stetson. Mutton-chop sideburns ran down his cheeks almost to his jaw.

Countless women had long ago decided that Spur McCoy was ruggedly handsome, just as men beyond number had been brought to justice through the actions of his mind, body and a variety of weapons. He was the best shot in the service.

After serving in Washington for six months, Spur had won the job of agent in charge of the entire west, from St. Louis all the way to the golden beaches of California.

He rarely heard from the top man in the Secret Service, William Wood, who'd held down a desk job in Washington ever since being appointed by Abraham Lincoln. Every president since Lincoln had re-appointed him.

His direct superior in Washington, General Wilton D. Halleck, sent Spur on various assignments through that modern miracle—the telegraph.

McCoy's latest job was transporting and guarding two brand new dies—one for each face—of the $20 double eagle gold coin. He'd picked them up at the Denver Mint and was on his way to deliver them to its sister plant in San Francisco.

Security on the movement of the dies had been tight. To confuse anyone who might try to steal them, General Halleck had sent out two other couriers at the same time from the Denver mint in different directions. Only a few top men knew that Spur McCoy had the real dies.

No one, however, knew where he'd hidden them. Just hours before he was to leave Denver Spur had called at the home of a saddlemaker on the outskirts of town. He'd woken up the balding Prussian and told him he wanted a small, cloth-

wrapped metal box hidden inside the saddle Spur
had bought from him that very afternoon.

McCoy halted the man's protests and natural
curiosity by pressing a crisp $50 bill into his hand.
He told him that the box contained something very
precious to him and he wasn't about to lose it.

After stuffing the money into his pocket the man
had studied the saddle, searching for the best place
to secrete the goods. Done with this he ripped
seams, tearing into the saddle just deep enough to
allow the box's placement within it.

Finished, he restitched, pushing the heavy steel
needle through the thick leather with gloved
hands. His bald pate glistened in the warm light as
he worked to piece it back together.

After the minor saddle surgery Spur had
surveyed the Prussian's handiwork. The dies were
completely invisible. They should be safe until his
arrival in San Francisco—if he could hang on to the
saddle.

Spur had been given a circuitous route to the city
by the bay, hopping from one small town to
another, riding stage coaches for most of the way.
He was nearly halfway to his destination and had
had no problems—until that night.

McCoy snarled as he thought of the skinny, left-
handed man, of how he'd been forced to gun him
down. Spur had felt no satisfaction while killing
the drunken, knee-shaking coward. No sense of
power or glory had flooded through him as he'd
looked down at the dead man, only hollow relief
that he'd managed to guard the dies for one more
day.

Word of them had leaked out. No doubt about it.
The man certainly knew of them, and others
probably did as well. He could expect more trouble
along the way. Hell, he was willing to bet on it.

But how had he found out? Frowning, Spur
mentally checked the door—yes, he'd locked
it—rested his rifle over his chest, threw his hat
onto the floor and closed his eyes. He'd wonder
about that in the morning.

This wasn't going to be an easy assignment.

2

A bump stirred Spur to consciousness. He opened his eyes, coughed up a load of trail dust and looked out the tiny, square window. Endless miles of harsh, dry desert stretched out in a never-changing panorama of desolation.

He shifted his gaze to the women who sat across from him in the bouncing stagecoach. The two old biddies, their fat bodies wrapped in endless layers of stiff, black taffeta, stared balefully at him, eyes full of accusations. Beads of sweat squeezed out on their pale foreheads below wide-brimmed black sun bonnets.

Spur cursed to himself and turned back toward the window.

They'd been glaring at him like that ever since the stage had left Hastings, Arizona Territory at ten that morning. In an attempt to quell their loathing he'd tried to engage them in friendly conversation but the old hags had kept their lips and knees pressed tightly together, gripping their beaded purses before their huge bosoms as if to safeguard their womanhood.

Spur sighed. Easy conversation always made long trips more pleasant but he knew he wouldn't get that from these two biddies. They seemed convinced that he was eagerly waiting for the right

moment to jump them, rip their dresses and
shawls and corsets from their gross bodies and
plunge deep where (he was sure) no man had gone
before.

They glanced at each other, nodded and returned
their stares at him.

He smiled as the clattering, jolting stage passed
a stand of sagauro cactus. Hell, he had better
things to think about than two stopped-up old
women whose beauty, if indeed they'd ever
enjoyed it, had long ago died on the vine.

He thought of the morning. McCoy had slept
through the night without problems and had gone
into the dining room for breakfast. As the blonde-
haired, beautiful, hotel owner's daughter had
served him Spur fought off the urge to feast on the
firm nipples that poked through her high-necked
gingham dress. Instead of satisfying his bulging
crotch he'd filled his rumbling stomach with stacks
of flapjacks drowned in Vermont maple syrup,
sizzling bacon and freshly-laid eggs. He'd washed
down the hearty meal with two cups of strong,
bitter coffee that she poured from a stained metal
pot.

Afterward, though, when he was splashing cold
water on his stubbly chin to wash away spots of
dried egg yolk, a soft hand knocked on his door.
He'd wiped his face with a coarse towel and,
stripped to the waist, opened it.

The blonde-haired beauty's gaze lingered on his
chest before lifting to his face.

"I'm—I'm sorry, sir, but I was wondering if you
needed a—a—" A blush flooded through her
cheeks.

"A what?" Spur asked, surprised but delighted
at her boldness. She didn't seem the kind of girl
who'd come calling at a strange man's hotel room,

even if she worked there.

"A special sendoff?" she asked.

Then Spur saw the fire in her light green eyes, in her parted, dry lips. It must have been burning all morning. No wonder she'd given him seconds of anything he'd asked for. She nearly swooned.

He gripped the nameless girl's slender waist, feeling the tight corset beneath it, as she swayed beneath him on unsteady feet.

"Little lady, are you sure you—" Spur began.

"Take me!" she whispered, with surprising passion. "I've waited for this!"

Spur shut the door behind her. He wasn't about to ask any questions as she straightened up and rubbed her sleek flanks against his groin. Spur slammed his mouth down on hers as he ripped the pearl buttons from their cloth holes on the back of her dress. She moaned as he pushed his tongue between her soft lips and nuzzled it against her.

The blonde—McCoy never did learn her name— arched her back as he freed the last button and tore the high-waisted, gingham dress from the body.

Blood pounded into Spur's groin. The girl felt his erection as he pushed it against her soft crotch and ravished her mouth.

The dress slipped from her shoulders and arms and hit the floor. Spur pulled his lips from hers, stepped back and drank in her beauty.

Naked save for the tight white corset fastened around her waist the blonde girl's body was luscious—wide hips with a dark, mysterious patch between them; a narrow waist and creamy white breasts that jutted above her corset. The perfectly round, voluptuous hemispheres were so large that Spur knew he'd never fit them into his mouth. At least, not all of them.

His erection pressed painfully against his pants

as she looked up at him with wide green eyes, unashamed at her nakedness.

"Do I please you?" she asked timidly.

"Please me! Yes, hell yes!"

"Then what are you waiting for?"

"Hell!" What *was* he waiting for? McCoy bent and captured a hard, red nipple between his slick lips. He chewed on it softly, sending groans of desire shooting from the girl. Spur sucked half the breast into his mouth. He was aroused, hard, and ready for the girl's unexpected sexual offer.

"I can't wait any longer!" the blonde said, panting. "I've been watching you all morning, wondering how it looks, how it feels. Get that thing out!" Her eyes were wild with passion. "Take me now, mister! Ride me!"

Spur ripped open his fly, releasing his monster. The girl flushed as his huge erection swung up between his legs. It jutted out majestically from his hairy crotch.

"Land sakes!" the blonde said. "That's what I've been waiting for. Hell, it's *more* than I've been waiting for, more than I could imagine!" She dropped to the floor, laid on her back and lifted her hips, exposing her blonde vee.

McCoy walked to her, pushed his pants to his ankles and, in one swift, well-aimed motion, stretched out over her and slid his hard penis full-length into her slot.

She arched her back and squealed in delight as he filled her. Their pubic hairs intertwined as Spur moved gently back and forth inside her, opening her, stretching her as she'd never been stretched before, savoring the wet, tight sensations that flooded through him.

Lust shot through his body. Spur gripped her firm buttocks and pumped hard, fast, each plunge nearly taking her breath away as their hips bounced together.

Straining his neck Spur suckled her right breast, pushed it into his salivating mouth, lightly chewing on its hard tip as he worked over her moist, willing opening.

Long before he wanted to, long before he'd begun to satiate his sudden passion, McCoy felt excitement boil within him. He plunged harder, deeper into the young woman's yielding opening, until his frantic thrusts sent the blonde girl into a clenching orgasm.

"Yes! Yes!" she said. Her face and breasts flushed a bright red and her hips rose to meet his driving thighs.

Spur ejaculated deep within her, spurt after spurt, thrust after thrust.

Their slick bodies molded together as they shuddered through their climaxes. Spur, edging off from the brain-shattering experience, flopped down onto her slender form. He felt her heart pounding through her chest as his own matched it in speed and tempo.

Her mouth found his wet lips. They kissed, long, slow, lovingly, as waves of warm passion washed through them.

Hours later, Spur still relished the experience and enjoyed recalling it, but wondered about the left-handed drunkard who'd tried to steal the dies from him. How the hell had the man known about them, and that he had them? McCoy would never know.

He sighed and opened his eyes. The old woman to the left, the slightly less ancient of the pair, dabbed a lace handkerchief to her forehead, looked quizzically at his face, then glanced down.

Her thin, pale lips parted in surprise and shock.

"You . . . you *animal!*" she screamed, flinging the handkerchief at him. "Agnes, look! I knew it!" she shrieked.

As the second woman dropped her gaze Spur wondered what had caused the outburst, until he felt the familiar, erotic tightness between his legs. Memories of that extraordinary woman and her eagerness to please him and herself that morning had, understandably, aroused him.

He laughed at the two terrified women, crossed his legs and settled his hat over his face.

They wish, Spur mused.

Sunlight slanted harshly across the barren landscape as the stagecoach bounced nearer the pocket of civilization that was to be their stop for the night. Little River, Arizona Territory, was one of hundreds of similar small towns scattered throughout the west.

Not far from Mexico, the whole town consisted of two streets that intersected near a large, wooden building that housed the sheriff's office, the hotel and barber. Eight or nine other businesses—including the standard livery stable, saloon, bank and general store, lined the streets every five hundred feet or so. About a dozen ill-constructed houses and a central, tiled well completed the town's highlights, along with several dusty mesquite trees and a few straggly desert junipers.

Little River wasn't much more than a glorified stage stop, Spur mused as the driver reined in the sweating horses. The coach pulled to a stop before the hotel. He disembarked, retrieved his saddle and carpet bag from the top of the rickety stage, and surveyed his surroundings as the two old biddies gave him a wide berth on their way to the hotel.

Four horses solemnly drank at the water trough before the Cat's Eye Saloon. A young buck escorted his plain, humble wife along the dusty street. An aging cowboy enjoyed the porch shade on the ten feet of boardwalk that fronted the general store.

Spur thought of his supply of cash. He may be carrying priceless dies but he had to think of the immediate future. He was nearly out of small change and, since the town was graced with a bank, McCoy figured he might as well try breaking a twenty.

Hauling the saddle over his back with one hand and the well-worn carpet bag with the other, Spur walked the short distance to the squat, ugly building and strolled inside.

"What the hell you want?" a nervous-eyed, gaunt man asked as he looked up from his ledger.

"Change." Spur clipped the word. He set down the bag and yanked a well-crumpled twenty-dollar bill from his pocket, unfolded it and handed it to the man who sat behind the hardwood desk.

The man frowned and examined the bill as if he'd never seen one before.

"This is a bank, or did I read the sign wrong?"

"Hell yes this is a bank!" The black-suited, string-tied man grunted and walked to the safe at the back of the small, plain office, clutching the twenty. "Cain't be too careful," he said, spinning the tumblers swiftly in several directions before opening the large iron door.

Spur grimaced as the man stuck his head inside the well-guarded cavity. Friendly town, he mused.

'I kin give you ones."

"Okay. Fine."

The man quickly returned with the change and threw it onto the desk. "Count it yerself," he said gruffly, plopping down into the chair. "I got work to do." The banker bent over his stained, scrawl-covered ledger and dipped his pen into the splattered ink well.

Spur retrieved the stack of bills and counted them carefully. "Thanks for your friendly consideration," he said.

"Git yer ass outa here!" the man thundered.

Spur chuckled as he folded and pocketed the bills. He left the bank and turned toward the hotel to get a flop for the night.

A lone rider quietly entered Little River well after dusk. The man had pulled his hat brim down low, over his eyes as he tied up his frothing, slick horse at the hotel's hitching post. He quickly rubbed her down, soothing her tired, aching muscles. The horse drank deeply and whinnied as he slapped her left flank. He was almost as tired as she was.

Maybe tonight, the figure mused, as he turned for the hotel. Maybe tonight he'd get them. If not he could wait. He done a lot of that so far—two week's worth.

After all, it was a sure thing.

The bullet hit the bottle, shattered it and sent whiskey and deadly splinters of glass showering down on the saloon table. Spur pushed back his chair and dove under the stained table. He squatted beside his saddle as another bullet zinged overhead through the saloon.

"I'm fuckin' mad!" a brusque voice needlessly announced.

Spur looked questioningly through the table legs at the man who'd squatted with him and suddenly realized he'd dropped his cards in the excitement.

"Don't worry about ol' Sam," the snaggle-toothed young man said.

"I'm not worried, just wonderin'." He'd been well into a good game of poker with the kid—the one he'd seen squiring around his plain wife when he'd arrived in Little River—when the firearm had sounded and broken up the game.

"Don't blow up the place again, Sam!" the barkeep barked. "You'll pay for every goddamned bottle you shoot! And you damn well better be able to afford it!"

An ear-splitting explosion and subsequent shatter told Spur that Sam had racked up another charge.

"What's gotten him so riled up?" Spur asked the card-clutching man across the table from him as the scent of gunpowder and blue smoke surrounded them.

"Hell, I dunno. It doesn't take much. Happens about once a week. He drifted into town a few months back." The kid grinned. "Why'n you duck back up and git yer cards?" the toothy youth suggested. "No sense in lettin' him ruin our game. I'm gonna empty your pockets, stranger!"

What the hell. Spur poked his head above the table and grabbed the cards, got a quick look at the big, red-faced man, who stood reloading beside the bat-wing doors, then returned to the relative safety of the floor.

"Heck, Buck—he's this saloon's apron—he ain't mad. Sam gives him more business'n the rest of us." The youth glanced at his cards. "Where wus we?" he asked, scratching his head. "Your raise or mine?"

Spur couldn't remember.

After the trigger-happy fool had gone, Spur returned to his drab room for some shut-eye. He surveyed the surroundings and quickly realized he was vulnerable there. The door had a lock but he had been given no key. Additionally, the room was on the ground floor and there wasn't a chair he could push under the door knob.

At that hour the cheery Mexican hotel keeper would be well into his *siesta*. Spur laid on the bed and tried to relax, but figured he wouldn't get any sleep until he was again on the stage.

Two hours later, however, he'd dropped off. Spur tossed on the lumpy mattress, sweating, his brain crammed full of disgusting images of those two old hags from the stagecoach forcing him to sexually service them.

The nightmarish scenes quickly dissolved and he woke to full consciousness as he felt a cold, round steel object pressing into his mouth.

3

Spur automatically started to struggle in his darkened hotel room, then lay still as he focused his eyes. He was staring down the eight-inch barrel of an old Army revolver. The muzzle inched closer to his throat.

"Think twice about giving me any trouble," its owner said, and laughed. "Nothing'd please me more than pulling this trigger and watching your head split open. You just lie still. Okay?" he asked.

Spur nodded toward the man. In the darkened room he couldn't see the face but the voice was vaguely familiar. Spur cursed himself at being caught in this situation but he relaxed. It wasn't over yet.

The gunman eased the barrel out. Spur flinched as the fixed sight scraped along the roof of his mouth before flopping past his upper lip.

"Talk," the man said, keeping the revolver trained between Spur's eyes. "What'd you put in the bank this afternoon?"

Spur shook his head. "Nothing. I just changed a twenty-dollar bill."

"Bullshit!" the man said, exploding with fury.

"It's true," Spur said. "Go ask the guy for yourself. You got any more questions? I need my sleep."

27

The man laughed hollowly. "I'll give you some sleep—eternal sleep if you don't tell me the truth!" He jabbed the 8-inch barrel between McCoy's eyes.

Spur thought quickly. His holster wasn't where he'd hung it over the bedpost. The man must have stashed it somewhere. A glint of steel near the door told him that it was well out of reach. Think, he told himself. Think to save your ass!

"You must have me mistook for someone else, mister. I didn't put anything in the bank. Hell, I'm leaving on the stage in the morning. I've been wandering around looking around for a place to settle down and happened to end up in this dusty excuse of a town. I don't know what you want, but you've got the wrong fuckin' man!" Spur spread innocent indignation over his hard, planed face.

"Good story—but not good enough." He poked the barrel against Spur's forehead, pressing it against the skin. "Talk, asshole!"

"You want my money? I—I put it in my saddle. Everything you want's in there." He motioned to the saddle that the man had placed against the wall under the solitary window.

"Everything I want?" He grunted. "Maybe you are telling me the truth," he said. "But I ain't gonna go over there and get it. We're gonna go. Move, fuck-head!" he growled. "Sit up nice and easy like."

With the cold steel digging into his forehead, Spur rose to a sitting position.

"Slowly, asshole, slowly swing yer skinny legs to the edge of the bed. Try anything and I'll blow your brains out!"

He stared into the man's beady, shining eyes and nodded. Pressing his hands on either side of him on the soft mattress, Spur lifted his booted legs, violently swung them up and smashed them into the man's mid-section.

A howl of surprise shot up from the man. He lifted the revolver. Spur knocked it from his hand with a solid, hard punch, drove his right fist into the shadowed man's stomach and another to his chin.

The big man doubled over as Spur sprung to his feet and drove his knee against the prominent chin, sending the man reeling backward.

Spur dove for the Army revolver, slid along the warped floorboards and felt the satisfying slap of the gun's walnut stock in his hand. He spun around on his hips just in time to see the dark, groaning figure crash through the window.

Spur rose and stared out. Nothing. The man wasn't in sight. McCoy checked the deserted streets once again and then looked down at the handsome .44. He turned it over in his hands. Nice piece, he thought; not as fine as a genuine Remington '58 but not bad.

He looked out the broken window again. The town was small, there couldn't be more than two hundred or so people there, but they weren't the friendliest folks he'd met.

He was sure no one had seen or heard anything that would lead to his finding the would-be bandit. Spur weighed his natural urge to stalk the man with his main job—moving the dies safely to San Francisco.

McCoy sighed. He'd let the bandit go. Besides, the man hadn't mentioned the dies. He'd just wanted his money. For all he knew it was old Sam, the one who'd shot up the saloon, looking for funds to pay off the barkeep.

Yeah, the voice had sounded vaguely familiar, but Spur had spent the better part of three hours in the saloon that night. He'd probably heard every male Little River resident talking, boasting or swearing in that time.

So he'd gotten a revolver out of the night's entertainment and a sore mouth. He coughed and shook his head. He wouldn't miss Little River when the coach pulled out of there in the morning.

The ride to Juniper was uneventful. The two sexless, sex-crazed hags had, fortunately, decided to stay an extra day in Little River, presumably deciding to risk another twenty-four hours in the rough town than a second close-quarters ride with McCoy.

When the coach stopped in Juniper just after dark to change horses, Spur got off. Sneezing and spitting eight hours of dust from his lungs and nose, he hauled his 28-pound saddle and carpet bag to the nearest saloon, The Fancy Garter. Juniper was a larger town than Little River, Spur thought, though he didn't see much of it in the dark. He slid through the batwing doors, sidled up to the crowded bar and ordered a whiskey from the scar-faced bartender.

He downed half of the cracked glass's contents in one gulp. As the bitter, woodsy liquid poured down his throat and warmed his insides Spur glanced around the room.

Three poker games were in session. Two cowboys, surrounded by empty whiskey bottles, snored loudly from a table's slick, alcohol-covered surface.

A fourth table was occupied by a brassy-haired, big-bosomed woman packed into a red and white, tight-waisted, puff-sleeved dress.

Interested, Spur studied her. She was no saloon girl, he decided. The redhead lacked the tired, list-

less look that most of the *Pistol Packing Peggys*
and *Squirrel Faced Shirleys* carried as they used
their thighs to squeeze as much cash out of as
many lonely men as they could.

Maybe she'd had too much to drink and her man,
disgusted, had left her there to fend for herself.
Maybe she didn't have a man and thought she had
to dress that way to attract one. Spur certainly
wasn't complaining as he looked her up and down,
but he wondered why none of the other men had
jumped her yet.

Maybe they had and she was just resting,
though she looked fresh enough.

The blue-eyed beauty saw him, smiled and
eagerly tapped her table. Maybe he was wrong.
Spur motioned for her to wait and, carrying his
saddle and carpet bag in one hand, walked to the
bar to get a fresh whiskey.

"Who's the filly?" he asked the scar-faced
barkeep.

"Hell if I know." The man refilled his glass.
"Lena something. Been coming around here for a
week, always drunker than a skunk. Never seen her
before that." He spit a long brown stream of
tobacco juice onto the floor.

Spur paid the man and walked to her. She smiled
broadly as he set down his glass and tipped his
Stetson. "Ma'am," he said.

"Sit down, go ahead, sit down!" the woman said
eagerly—too eagerly.

He obliged, dropped his saddle and bag to the
floor and grabbed his whiskey. He took a healthy
gulp.

"Lena Mac Dougal," she said, offering her hand.

"Frank Burch." He automatically used his cover
name as he pressed her hand.

"You're not from around here, are you?" she

asked. "I never forget a face."

"Nope. Just arrived a few minutes ago. What's a nice girl like you—"

The brassy-haired beauty laughed. "Brother, whaddya think I'm doing here?" Her blue eyes sparkled, her painted lips were a bit loose and her cheekbones were rosy.

She was drunk.

"You don't work here, do you?" Spur bluntly asked. Something about this otherwise delectable woman made him vaguely uneasy.

"I work where I want to." Her voice was defensive as she pouted and adjusted her breasts with a delicate, white hand. "Buy a girl a drink?" she asked lasciviously.

Spur laughed. She'd fooled him. "Sure." He started for the bar but stopped when she gripped his hand.

"Not here. My place."

Lena stood, offering him her left arm. They walked out of the saloon as Spur dragged his saddle and carpet bag with his left hand.

They moved down the boardwalk. Juniper, Arizona Territory, was preparing for the night. Lamps had been lit throughout the town, creating a fantasy of white, yellow and golden shimmering lights.

"Seriously, what are you doing in this place?" Spur asked, enjoying the cool night air and the feel of the young woman's hand on his arm.

"Just passing through on my way to Frisco. I've taken stage coaches and trains since St. Louis. I never intended to even stop here but one of the horses had thrown a boot and, well, after they got it back on his foot I somehow seemed to get stuck here."

"Shoe."

"I beg your pardon?"

"Horses have shoes, not boots."

"Oh." She giggled. "I'm really a city girl," she explained. "I don't know a lot about horses."

"Keeping busy out here?"

She turned to him and smiled. "You might say that. Lots of lonely men here in Juniper. Why, I wouldn't dream of leaving just yet."

He smirked. "Must give you a warm feeling inside, knowing you're helping out all those poor men."

"Oh yes; I come from a long line of charity workers." The laugh rippled from her painted lips as they entered her hotel.

Once in her room, the red-haired woman sat on her bed and began undressing. "You still haven't told me anything about yourself, Frank Burch." Her voice was faintly accusing.

"Neither have you."

Spur leaned against the door, arms crossed over his broad chest. He'd enjoy watching her remove every article of clothing almost as much as he would seeing her without them on.

Lena smiled, struggling with her dress buttons. "You know all about me—I'm a working girl spreading love and affection throughout this great land. Now tell me what you do. You're no drummer, are you?"

Spur laughed. "No. Guess again."

She sized him up. "You don't look like a bank robber."

He shook his head.

"I give up—on you and these darn buttons."

"Let me help you."

He moved to her then, sat beside the woman and undid her dress. Their thighs pressed together.

"Oh no!" she said as her dress fell forward into

her hands. She pushed it against her body.

"What? Having second thoughts? Think I can't pay you or something?"

Lena shook her head and searched his eyes. "You —you aren't some kind of *lawman* or something, are you?"

Spur smiled. "No," he lied. "What makes you ask that? Do I look like a lawman?"

"I don't know."

"You have something against lawmen?"

Lena smiled and stood, dropping the dress to the floor. She was completely nude. No chemise, bloomers or petticoats obscured her body. The soft kerosene light illuminated her curves, fuzzy groin and pink nipples.

"No. It's just that—well, daddy was a lawman. In St. Louis. And—and ever since I—"

"I see."

He didn't know what she was talking about, but he certainly did see her—all of her. When she stood before him, however, Spur again sensed something was wrong. He realized what it was when she pushed her hand between his legs.

Lena frowned at what she felt. "Hell, boy, what's the matter with you? Aren't I pretty enough?" she said, massaging his limp bulge.

"No. I mean yes, hell yes you're pretty. Prettiest thing I've seen in a long time." He looked down at her busy hand. "I don't know. Maybe I'm just tired. I've been traveling for a long time."

"Yeah? Where are you headed, Frank?"

She redoubled her efforts, stroking, massaging, running her tongue in and out of his ear, but it didn't work. He was as limp as a dry sheet in the breeze.

"Nowhere in particular. Just wandering around, looking for a place to settle down."

The woman continued her efforts for a few minutes, furiously trying to stir lust into his groin. When it was clear that it wasn't going to work she finally sat beside him.

"Look, boy, I don't know what your problem is," she said angrily. "Maybe you've been spending too much time with your horse."

Damn! Spur thought. Why the hell couldn't he give her what he'd given so many other women? Maybe it was something about the girl, something he just didn't like. "I don't have a horse—not here, anyway."

"I guess you're not gonna have me neither." Lena unpinned her hair, shook it back and ran a hand over her forehead. She frowned. "It coulda been good, Frank. It coulda been real good. I'm the best there is."

"I can believe it." He stood and shrugged. "Maybe some other time."

"When you leaving Juniper?" she asked, a curious urgency in her words.

"In the morning."

"Well, okay, be that way." She pouted again. "I hope you fall off your danged horse!"

"I don't—" Spur sighed, picked up his belongings and walked out of the room, leaving the frustrated girl sitting stark naked on her bed.

Spur didn't really mind, though he couldn't remember such a thing happening to him more than a few times in his long, sweat-packed, body-bucking history. That woman was more than she appeared to be, he thought, and somehow it had bothered him—even that part which was rarely bothered by anything.

He put it out of his mind. Time he checked into a hotel, ate and played some poker. He might as well enjoy himself on this job.

Besides, he realized, as the hard leather saddle straps cut into his shoulder, there were millions of women out there waiting for him. He didn't mind disappointing one of them.

Much.

4

"Lawson, honey, I'm sorry!" the tear-streaked woman said. "I tried my best but he wouldn't tell me a damn thing! Hell, he wouldn't even screw me!"

The burly, six foot-one, black-haired man raised his hand again, sending the fully-dressed woman cringing against the far end of his hotel room bed. She stared up at him from lowered lashes, panting. A bright pink spot on her left cheek showed the result of his last slap.

"You tried!" he thundered. "That's not good enough, not with all this at stake!" He stared down at her, fuming, threatening her again and again with another hard slap. Finally he lowered his hand. "Damn! I shoulda known he wouldn't tell you anything. He's too smart for that."

His hard brown eyes softened as he gazed at the beautiful, buxom woman who cowered against the iron headboard. "Did I hurt you much?" Lawson Amory's voice was suddenly tender.

The red-haired woman pouted and rubbed her shining cheek with slender, white fingers. "No. Not much. I've had worse. Lots of men have slapped me around." She sniffed.

"Look, Lena, I'm sorry. I figured you—of all the women in this damned town—could get anything you wanted out of him. Guess I was wrong."

Lena MacDougal wiped her cheeks, visibly relaxing now that the danger of another solid blow had passed. "He wouldn't tell me nothing, not a word about what he's doing here."

Lawson nodded. "Did you feel his pockets like I told you to?"

"Yeah, I felt his pockets—I felt all over between his legs." Lena half-smiled. "He didn't have anything in his pockets except for what felt like a wad of money." Her blue eyes focused on his. "What do you want from him, anyway, Lawson? It can't be that. You've got tons of money."

"Yeah, what I haven't given you." Amory laughed shortly. "Hell, don't worry your pretty little head about it. I knew it'd be hard."

Her eyes lit up. "I hope it's hard. Hell, that guy couldn't get it up if a dozen girls lifted their skirts and stuck their behinds into his face!" Lena smiled. "You're more of a man than him. I think he's partial to horses!"

Amory smiled at the insult. The girl's passion was infectuous; he felt a tightening in his crotch. "Come on over here, gal! I won't hurt you again."

Lena squealed delightedly and rolled across the bed until she bumped against his muscled thigh.

"Get to work," he said harshly as she gazed up at him. "I'm paying you so I might as well enjoy it."

"Yes sir!"

Lena MacDougal fumbled with his fly, ripped it open, pushed her hands past his shorts and hauled out his rising organ. She slipped it's hard, mushroom-shaped head into her mouth and moaned.

A rush of warmth flooded through Lawson Amory as he forced himself deeper into the woman.

Enjoy yourself, he thought, as Lena started to work him over. He'd have to bide his time. Didn't want to risk a confrontation with the man here.

Lawson Amory allowed himself to relax as he

enjoyed the woman's mouth. Hell, he could wait.
He relished the satisfaction of knowing that long
before Spur McCoy could board that ship for San
Francisco the dies would be his and the Secret
Service agent would be lying in a puddle of blood.

He'd enjoy watching the man die.

The sun hung directly overhead, burning the
desert into an arid wasteland. The Butterfield
Express stagecoach rattled down a dusty, rude
trail through the desolation as it moved toward
Clover, the next town along the line. The vast,
barren landscape stretched out to infinity around
it.

Bizarre rock formations lay strewn over the
ground up ahead. They rose hundreds of feet into
the air—twisted, broken pinnacles of long-dead
mountains worn down by centuries of sand and
wind.

Inside, the heat was oppressive. It radiated from
the ceiling overhead and in through the windows.
Dust-laden air hung around the four men seated
there.

"Indians," the black-suited man said. He sat
beside Spur in the bouncing stage. "I know they're
out there."

"You worried?" McCoy lazily asked the man.
They'd been talking about the dangers of the
untamed countryside to pass the time.

"Hell no! No sense in worrying about what
might be." Bart Clemons mopped his slick, dust-
coated forehead with a stained handkerchief and
stuffed it back into his pocket. "I'm just curious.
Never seen real live Indians before."

"Injuns, hell!" The unshaven cowboy seated
across from Spur lit up a cheroot with a sulphur
match and inhaled the bitter smoke. "Let me at
'em. I'll blast those soulless devils to hell! They're

lower 'n animals!"

"They're not soulless devils, asshole, they're human beings," Ted Malbrough said. The thin, bearded salesman stared out the window. "As much as ah hate to admit it, they have ev'ry right to attack us."

"How you figure that, Malbrough?" Clemons asked.

His thin lips bent into a harsh smile. "We took their land, slaughtered their people, stripped their huntin' grounds, burned their fields and took away their religion. Those that still got breath in 'em are just trying to stay alive, and ah don't blame 'em a bit!" The New Orleans salesman's accent was as thick as the silt-laden Mississippi River.

"Mighty high-faluting talk, drummer! But I still say they're soulless devils." The cowboy snorted and inhaled again, then blew out the smoke in perfect circles.

"Might as well keep a watch, just in case," Spur said, and looked out at the lonely countryside through the small black window.

The stage drew nearer to the mass of sharp, sheer rocks that jutted dramatically from the desert floor. The trail that wound through them looked vulnerable.

That'd be the best place to stage an attack, Spur thought. Plenty of prime hiding places in the broken cliffs above them, lots of spots to set up crack archers.

The six horses whinneyed as the driver urged them forward up the slanting road. Their hooves broke sharp rocks into dust as they strained against the increased weight.

"See anything?" Spur asked.

"Nope," Clemons answered, as he strained his neck out the opposite window.

"Hell, you worry too much!" the cowboy said. "I ain't afraid of no yellow-bellied Injuns!"

A sharp cry issued from above them.

"What in hell was that?" the banker asked.

Spur stuck his head out the window in time to see the driver's arrow-riddled body fall past him on its way to the ground.

"The driver. He's dead!" Spur said.

"Indians!"

The horses, suddenly freed from pressure on their reins, panicked. They surged forward, snarling and snorting, up the sloping trail. Clemons and Spur searched the overhead rocks from the bouncing windows.

"I don't see a plum thing!" Bart yelled.

"They have to be out there somewhere!" Spur strained his eyes but saw no movement, no Indians.

An arrow whizzed past. The slender wooden shaft dug two inches into the right rear horse's flank.

The mare screamed. Her pain-racked leg faltered, stumbled. The six teamed horses veered to the right, sending their pounding hooves into a deep gulley created by centuries of intermittent rainfall.

"Holy shit!" Malbrough said, clutching to the jerking seat.

The coach lurched sickeningly and jolted sideways as the horse's hooves caught in the deep slot, tangling their legs. It stopped suddenly. The wounded, whinneying horse fell to the ground, pulling the rest of the kicking, screaming team with it.

The Butterfield Express coach's left wheels shot into the air as the horses pulled vertically against it. The seat slanted sharply, slamming the cowboy and the drummer against Spur and Clemons.

"We're going over!" the banker yelled.

The coach teetered on its right, iron-wrapped wheels for five endless seconds before crashing onto its side with a bone-rattling crunch.

The four groaning men, piled on top of each other on the wall below them, tried to untangle their limbs as the horses snorted and groaned in agony from snapped ankles. The impact had knocked the breath out of Spur. He gasped, picked himself up and shook his head.

"Everyone all right?" he asked.

The three men yelled affirmitively.

"Git yer smelly boot outa my face, banker!" the cowboy said.

"I will if you get yours outa my back, cowboy!" came the retort.

Spur gripped his long-barreled Colt .45 and poked his head out the now overhead window.

A lone Indian rider crashed down the cliff toward them, whooping triumphantly, swinging his bow above his head as his horse slid along the incline.

Spur lined up his shot and waited until the brave was within thirty feet. Just as the man drew back his arrow McCoy fired, slamming a load of hot lead through his chest.

The surprised Indian slid backward off his mount as his heart exploded. He dropped to the gorund and lay motionless as his frightened mount charged forward down the hill and veered onto the trail.

Lucky shot, Spur thought, as he ducked down into the carriage. The three men were settling themselves on the coach's side which now served as the floor.

"How many of 'em?" Bart Clemons asked.

"Used to be one but you can bet yer ass there's more out there." His face was grim.

"What're we gonna do?" Malbrough asked, shaking, his lips tight.

"Get ahold of yourself, drummer! You and Clemons see if you can kick some firing holes through the floorboards. Do it now!"

The two men nodded as they squatted before it.

They pounded their boots against the warped surface.

"Hurry, goddamn it!" Clemons said.

Spur turned to the cowboy, who sat slumped against the floor rubbing his jaw. "Where's your big words now, cowboy? I thought you were going to take care of the Indians singlehanded."

The sullen man fixed his eyes on the bright window opposite him.

The men pounded the dilapidated floor with their thick-soled boots. The old, felt-covered wood took the force at first, then buckled, splintered and cracked. Seconds later sunlight shone through four holes.

"Good enough. I sure hope you boys can use those things," Spur said, as the two men drew their weapons.

"Now's as good a time as any to find out!" Clemons checked his revolver.

Dozens of hooves pounded the hard-packed desert floor outside, growing nearer and louder, as the whole Indian raiding party approached them.

"Land sakes!" Clemons said. "Here they come!"

"Then stick your weapons through those holes and get ready to fire. This thing ain't over yet!"

5

The overturned Butterfield stagecoach seemed to grow even hotter as the four men huddled in it. Clemons and Malbrough, squatting and pressing their noses against the floor, peered through the firing holes they'd kicked through it.

Spur slid a sixth round into his .45. "What's the count?" he barked as the sounds of the approaching Indians grew louder. "How many of them?"

"Jesuz!" the salesman said. "Must be hundreds of 'em comin' down the cliff!"

"You're plumb crazy, Malbrough!" Bart Clemons said. "I see five—six of them."

"Anyway, there's more of them than us. Ah don't like them odds, not one bit."

"Quit yer bellyaching and use those guns!" Spur thundered.

The cowboy, who'd sat slumped in the corner since the coach had rolled over, jumped to his feet.

"I gotta get outa here!"

"Sit your butt down!" Spur said.

"No. I can do it. I can make it." The cowboy gripped the window above him and stuck his head fully through the hole.

"Shit-for-brains!" Clemons yelled.

Malbrough peeled off a shot at the approaching Indians, using a higher hole for sighting.

The cowboy screamed and dropped from the

overhead window onto the floor. A feathered arrow had turned his left eye into a mass of blood and tissue.

"Hell!" Spur snarled as he looked at the bleeding, mortally wounded man. The arrow had slammed into his brain, lodging deep inside the vital organ. "Had to go and get yourself killed!"

The cowboy's lanky body shook. His boots rattled on the wall beneath him as he gurgled out a scream. Moments later he lay silent.

Outside, loud whoops surrounded the coach. The Indians were closing in for the kill.

Malbrough blasted a bullet through the cracked floorboards. "Got one!" he shouted in joy.

Arrows rained down around them and slammed into the coach with dull thuds. One flew in through the window but fell harmlessly beside Spur's feet.

"Five to go," Clemons said, squatting.

Spur straddled the dead cowboy's body and lifted his fully-loaded .45. Pressing it against his chest he pushed his head and the Colt out through the window.

Spur lined up a shot. His .45 spoke and tore a hole through an approaching Indian's chest. The man howled, dropped his bow and bent forward on his mount. Just as McCoy ducked down into the coach again he saw the Indian flop to the ground.

"Good work!" the banker yelled at Spur. "That's four to go!"

Clemons and Malbrough fired repeatedly, furiously, filling the cramped coach with blue smoke and resounding explosions. Sweat squeezed from their foreheads as they alternately reloaded and struggled to sight the Indians as they circled on their prancing, saddleless mounts.

Repeated whacks told of dozens more arrows piercing the stage coach.

"Hold still, damnit!" Malbrough yelled.

"Yeah, make it easy for us!" the banker said sarcastically. "You think they're gonna line up?"

As Spur looked up at the window, ready to rise through it, the whole door above him suddenly swung open. Spur fired at the leering Indian as the man sent an arrow flying into the stagecoach. The strangled cry told him he'd hit his mark. The Indian slid off the coach.

Spur ducked back up through the opened door and quickly killed a fourth Indian.

"Damn. Sweet Jesus! I'm dying, man I'm dying! That bastard got me!"

Spur shot a look behind him. Bart Clemons lay against the wall, his face a mask of agony and terror. The hastily fired arrow had torn open his gut. Half its length stuck out from the banker's stomach.

"Damn! It hurts!" he howled, grasping the arrow with trembling hands.

"What—what do we do?" Malbrough asked. He gazed at the wounded man.

Gut wound, Spur thought. Nothing much they could do about it here. If they were in town maybe a doctor could patch him up. Here, miles from civilization, the Dodge City banker was doomed to a slow, painful death.

"What do we do?" Malbrough asked again, twisting his head from the groaning man to Spur.

He slowly shook his head. "Pray, drummer. Pray that you're not next."

"Can't we take that arrow outta him?" the man asked, his face white. "We gotta do something. We gotta!"

"No. The damage's been done." He shook his head again and hardened his voice. No time to waste. "Just get to work with that hogleg of yours."

He blocked out Clemon's screams. Two more to go. Just two Indians between life and death.

The banker's agonized groans increased in

volume. Marbrough hadn't moved. "I said forget
about it," Spur said. "Spit some lead at those
damned Indians!"

"Okay, you heartless bastard!" Marlbrough
moved to the holes again.

Sudden fury poured through Spur's veins. He
stood upright through the opened door and blasted
two rounds at the arrow-wielding Indians. At ten
yards the shots were easy. Seconds later both fell
to the ground, moaning, dying as the hot desert
sun shone on their blood-spurting wounds.

Glancing quickly around the area, Spur counted
seven dead, including the first he'd killed.
Adrenaline ran through him as McCoy sat down
and sighed.

Bart Clemons spluttered near his feet. His
wounded belly rose and fell like a roaring sea
around the murderous arrow. The banker's vital
organs, ripped and torn, poured poison throughout
his system.

The dying man looked at Spur. "Hell, guess it's
time I cashed in anyway." He managed a short,
wrinkled smile before wincing again as pain shot
through his body.

"You're gonna be fine," Spur lied, smelling fresh
blood. "We'll get you to a sawbones and—"

"Don't bullshit me!" Clemons said, and groaned.
He nodded with his chin. "They all dead?"

McCoy nodded.

The man closed his eyes. "Then git yer butts
outta here and let me die in peace. I don't need a
goddamned audience."

A new wave of intense pain flooded through the
banker. He doubled up and rolled onto his side as
he rode it out.

Ted Malbrough squatted before Clemons,
breathing heavily, his eyes wide and round.

"C'mon, Ted. Least we can do is give this man
his last wish."

The man looked up wildly, his lips parted, then nodded.

After checking to ensure that all seven Indians were dead and not just unconscious or lying in wait, Spur put the wounded coach horses out of their misery. All six soon lay dead on the sand.

The dead Indian's mounts had scattered across the desert and were nowhere in sight. Spur realized that he and the salesman had a long walk ahead of them.

He retrieved his carpet bag and saddle from where they'd been lying on the ground since the accident and hauled them a hundred yards away. Ted Malbrough was sitting there, silently, since they'd left the stage.

As they waited outside, ignoring the banker's agonized screams, the drummer got his bag of fixings and tried to roll a cigarette. His thin hands shook so much that he'd emptied half his tobacco onto the ground before successfully finishing the simple task. He struck a sulphur match and was soon puffing away on the stick.

Watching a light breeze scattering countless, tiny grains of sand against each other, Spur pushed all thoughts of the dying man and the attack out of his mind. San Francisco, he told himself, mulling over his assignment.

Two hours later the stagecoach was finally silent. Clemon's death screams had ended as he drifted into unconsciousness and eternal oblivion.

The two men outside sat quietly, paying their last respects.

"He—he dead?" Malbrough's voice was barely a whisper as he blew out a thin stream of acrid smoke.

"Yeah."

Ted's eyebrows crunched together as he glanced at the man sitting across from him. "Ah ain't used

to this. Never seen nobody die before. First the
cowboy and now Clemons."

"Maybe you'll be lucky and won't see it again."
He sighed. "Come on, we have work to do."

"Work?" the young man asked, taking a last
puff before tossing the smoke behind him.

Spur's voice was grim. "We're not leaving until
we've given those men a proper burial. Even the
cowboy deserves that much."

Malbrough nodded.

Using a small shovel they found in the wreckage
of the coach, the two men took turns digging
through the soft sand. Harsh sunlight made them
sweat until their clothes hung on them.

The heat radiated up from the ground, baking
them. Spur's throat ached. He needed a drink of
something—anything.

He called a rest. They found two canteens on the
coach. The men slaked their thirst and returned to
the work.

Soon they'd managed to dig two shallow graves.
They hauled out Clemons first and quickly covered
him over with sand, then the cowboy.

They hadn't spoken to each during the entire
time. As they stood staring down at the sandy
mounds, Spur wiped his forehead and sighed.

"Ain't ya gonna say something?" Malbrough
asked. "Shouldn't we read a Bible verse?"

"Know any?" he asked.

The man shook his head.

"Neither do I. Then we're done. The next stage
stop shouldn't be more'n six miles or so. Passed
one not long before the attack."

The drummer stood and stuffed his canteen into
his black leather luggage. "Ah ain't goin' with
you."

"Why in hell not, Malbrough?"

He frowned, wrinkling his slick, salty face.
"Hell, ah shouldn't be out here. Realized it when

those Indians attacked us. This ain't my place, so ah'm going back to Juniper, get the first stage ah can, and head home. Ain't gonna stop for nothing 'till ah see the Mississippi again."

Spur grunted. "Don't blame you. Best of luck, Malbrough."

The drummer nodded and turned toward the trail.

McCoy packed his canteen, slung the heavy saddle over his shoulder, gripped his carpetbag and started out down the trail as the sun slanted further before him.

The stage stop couldn't be too far away. He should get there long before dark.

Spur was well aware of his vulnerability. He was alone, on foot, with little water and no food, travelling through Indian territory. But he was alive and the dies were still safe. Things could be worse.

He walked relentlessly, following the crude trail, his boots kicking up clouds of dust. The harsh sunlight worked on him as it had on the desert for untold thousands of years.

The ground pounded below him. The trail beckoned for Spur to follow it toward the distant stage stop. The heat made his head light.

Hours later he stopped to rest under a cliff that provided welcome shade. He dribbled a bit of water onto his tongue and relished the liquid before gulping it down.

He leaned back against the cool rock wall and slowed his breathing. A pair of scorpions slithered across the sand. They halted, startled at the smell of human sweat. Raising their poisonous, curled tails, the pair threatened him for a moment, then thought better of it and scurried beneath a mass of dead cactus. Moments later he continued his journey.

For two hours Spur saw no living thing save for

a coyote cub who'd lost his mother and a few hawks riding the updrafts, training their keen eyes on the landscape in their endless search for prey.

The secret service agent flexed his mind as he strained his muscles, planning out each day that lay before him until he reached San Francisco and delivered the priceless package to the mint.

For the thousandth time Spur wondered how the news of the dies—especially the fact that he was moving them—had leaked out. The drunkard who'd yelled at him from the dark alley in Hastings damn well knew what he was transporting. But how had he known?

He shook his head, sending salty droplets onto the hot sand where they sizzled and evaporated. The man wouldn't cause him any futher trouble but he knew that others certainly would. He sighed, then McCoy fixed an image of San Francisco in his mind—the glittering lamps along the bay, the dark blue water lapping against tall ships, the bracing scent of sea water and the fancy ladies with smouldering eyes and tight satin dresses who invited with a flick of their eyelashes.

The picture soon faded as he hiked up a steep, rock-strewn incline. For the next hour he passed dozens of these rises. McCoy knew that they'd been carved out of the desert floor by infrequent, heavy rainstorms that had dumped their fury on the usually arid landscape. The rain had gathered and roared through the area, flooding masses of runoffs seeking the lowest point. As they surged across the sand they'd gouged deep gulleys as testimony to their primeval presence.

He struggled up another one. The next ridge, he kept telling himself, as his legs ached and his shoulder throbbed. Over the next one he'd see the stage stop.

Then, finally, as he gained its top, he saw the building far ahead. The tiny corner of human habitation shimmered in the intense heat. It was an oasis of civilization where food, water and rest waited.

McCoy redoubled his efforts, crashing down the sloping ground, nearly tripping over his feet. At the bottom he lugged the saddle onto his right shoulder, gripped his carpetbag with his left hand and pumped his legs hard.

His sweat-soaked clothes hung from his lean body. His head pounded from the intolerable heat. His chest painfully heaved, but he was almost there.

The stage stop dropped out of sight behind a small range of cracked mountains. As he continued his journey, snorting super-heated air through his nostrils and exhaling explosively through his mouth to nourish his aching lungs, Spur detected a bitter scent in the air. Woodsy. Spicy. The unmistakeable odor of smoke.

The aroma sent McCoy's stomach churning. Food. Someone was cooking in the now-invisible stage stop. Beans and steak and coffee and apple pie. He could almost taste them.

Slow down boy, he told himself. Think about getting hungry when you're there. Besides, the smoke didn't smell right. It seemed stale, old.

Twenty minutes later Spur stopped in his tracks, gazing at the stage stop that lay two hundred yards ahead. Even at this distance he realized that all was not right.

His worst fears had been realized. Though still standing, the small barn, squat wooden building, even the outhouse were laced with thick dark stripes of charcoal. Dead horses lay still on the ground. No humans moved there.

The stage stop had been burned.

6

Desolation surrounded him.

Spur dropped his saddle and carpetbag, slicked his forehead beneath his Stetson and stood in shock among the cold, charred remains of the stage stop. As he took in the scene of destruction and carnage, as the finality of it penetrated his brain, his nostrils flared. The acrid stench of burned human flesh rose up from the ground and hung in the air.

Near his feet lay the pitiful remains of four men, burned beyond recognition. A stagecoach lay in pieces beside the single-story structure. Arrows riddled the buildings. The troughs had been overturned, dooming the precious water to evaporate on the sand. Twelve horses lay heaped on each other, peppered with arrows, their huge eyes staring sightlessly out at the desert, their limbs twisted and broken.

Indians, he thought, and grimaced.

The fire they'd set—probably by overturning the cookstove—had barely scorched the surrounding land. Horses had apparently chewed nearby bushes and scrub to the ground, so the fire hadn't spread. Not far away lay a thicket of cottonwoods and maybe, just maybe, water.

He surveyed the area. No survivors, no dead
Indians even. They must have stormed in and
attacked before the people had a chance to defend
themselves.

McCoy shook his head and moved laterally away
from the buildings, away from the gut-churning
stench of overcooked human meat. He dropped to a
squat, panting. He was almost too tired to compre-
hend the sight, too hot and thirsty to take it in.
Had he walked so far only to come to this?

He closed his eyes and breathed deeply until his
heart had returned to its normal pace and he'd
rested. First things first. He checked his canteen.
Almost half full. If he didn't find water he couldn't
start out on the desert, not alone, not in this heat.
He didn't know the local waterholes and couldn't
risk the trip.

He'd have to wait until the next stage plodded
up and hope he could get a ride.

Spur sighed as he rose and glanced again at the
dusty cottonwoods. Worth a try, he thought, and
started for them. He ignored the aching in his
boots as he covered the hundred yards to the area.

The trees grew thickly, their slender trunks
caked with years of desert grime. Not the slightest
breeze stirred the leaves or snaked the trunks back
and forth, but the branches arching overhead
cooled the air. McCoy walked into the welcome,
soothing shade.

Cottonwoods were always a good sign of water,
he remembered. In this place they could be his
salvation.

As he moved into the grove, small patches of
bright green appeared on the sand below him, not
cactus but some sort of small leafy plant. Encour-
aged, Spur eagerly walked on the soft sand. His
boots crushed dozens of fragile plants that had

eeked out survival in the grove.

Then he heard it just ahead—the refreshing trickle of water splashing on rocks, the sound of constant dripping, of liquid spilling into liquid: the miracle of the desert.

A spring, he thought, grunting and smiling to himself. Good place for a stage stop—at least, it had been.

A distinct, sharp intake of breath ten feet from him, a miniscule rattle of bushes, set Spur's mind in motion. He froze and turned his head toward the sound's apparent place of origin.

An innocent, three-foot patch of horehound stood in the dappled sunlight. It was still, dense, intensely green. He approached it.

Another gasp, another rattle. Someone was in there. Had he surprised an Indian?

"Don't—don't—!" the bush said.

Spur smiled. It was a woman. By god, a woman!

"I'm not going to hurt you, ma'am," Spur said, halting seven feet away. He put his hands on his hips and stared at the bush. "You believe me?"

"Yes, I—I do." The voice was high, strained.

"Fine. Now why don't you come out of there? I'm not an Indian."

Silence, rustling, then the bush gave birth. A tall, striking blonde woman rose from it, her chin high, eyes wild with fright. The checkered tatters hanging from her body showed the remains of a calico travelling dress. Her face was smudged with smoke and dirt, her hair matted with leaves.

Her aquamarine eyes glowed. "Thank god you're not an Indian!" she said, relieved.

"Frank Burch, ma'am," Spur tipped his hat.

"I—I'm Beverly Thomas." The woman stared at him as if she'd never seen a white man.

"You all right, Miss Thomas?" Spur approached

her, cautiously, slowly.

She nodded and smiled. The simple act seemed to transform her, and Spur was struck by the incomparable beauty that lay beneath the traces of dirt, smoke and leaves.

"I'm fine, Mr. Burch." She coughed. "Tired, scratched, hungry—but fine."

"You gonna come outa that bush?"

She looked down and blushed, then stepped toward him, freeing her feet from the tangle of soft green branches. "I'm not myself. Please excuse the way I look—" She halted her sentence and eyed him sardonically. "Listen to me! You'd think I was back in Boston!"

"No need to apologize," he said gently. "I understand. What happened?"

Her smile faded. "The Butterfield Stage had stopped here to change horses. We—me and Parson Thomas—had just finished eating. The parson was reading his bible, something in Revelations, I think. I—" she blushed deeply, coloring her soiled cheeks, then looked away. "I'd left him to go off to the bushes to, well, *you know.*"

Spur nodded.

Beverly looked at him timidly. "Anyway, I'd just ducked into some bushes on the edge of the cottonwoods when I heard these unworldly voices coming out of nowhere. Then, horses running. Lots of them. I didn't know what was going on so I just stayed where I was, crouching inside the bushes, and—and watched." She folded her hands before her and closed her eyes, brushing her high checkbones with long, blonde lashes.

"Look, Miss Thomas, if this is too painful for you, you don't have to tell me."

She looked up sharply at him. "I have to tell someone!" She bent down and plucked a handful of some nameless, tiny white flower. Clutching it, she took a deep breath. "The trees were in the way, but I saw Indians riding up. I'd never seen any before. The driver was yelling his head off and Parson Thomas dropped his bible as he tore out from the kitchen."

She took a deep breath and continued. "Before I knew it they were all dead—the preacher, the driver and the two old men who ran that place. I looked away in fright and disgust but I heard something fall over. As they rode off I saw the fire they'd started and—and—." She squeezed her eyes shut again. "And they'd set fire to the men! All of them! There were four men I'd eaten with, one of them a man of God, and they were burning like birch twigs." She shivered and looked at him again. "So I just stayed here, walking farther into the trees. I'm not going back out there. Ever!"

Spur nodded. "Well, Miss Thomas, I think you could call yourself powerfully fortunate." He thought of what they would have done to her.

"I know." She nodded, her eyes cold. "I count my blessings every time I remember what it looked like back there. I fondly recall the day I decided to leave Boston and look up Trevor in San Diego!" Color burnished her cheeks, the product of frustration and anger.

"I'm sorry, Miss Thomas."

Her light blue eyes softened. "Don't be. I knew it was dangerous travelling alone across the Territory of Arizona. And call me Bev, not Miss Thomas. Okay?"

He nodded. Even though she'd been through hell, Spur couldn't help but notice that her dress had nearly slipped off her firm, rounded body. His eyes darted down quickly. "You have anything else you can wear?"

She paled and laughed, vainly trying to cover up
the large patches of bloomers and chemise that
showed plainly through torn checkerboard dress.
"My heavens! I'd forgotten that I was nearly
naked!" Bev laughed joyously. "Leave it to a man
to take a girl's mind off her troubles. Yes, I have
two bags, but they're out there." She pointed
toward the burned stage stop. This slight motion
ripped apart the few threads that held up the right
shoulder of her dress. It dropped down, revealing a
portion of her smooth, white upper shoulder and
the top of her chemise.

She giggled. "Oh hell!" Beverly slapped a
delicate, lightly scratched hand over her lips.
"Whoops! You probably think I'd be mortified to
be seen in this condition—and by a man at that.
But with all I've been through, it just doesn't
matter anymore. Not at all!"

He liked her. Spur was entranced by this dirty
but beautiful blonde. He admired her courage and
her openness. "I'd better go get your bags before
that dress falls off." He flashed her a wink and
turned toward the burned buildings.

"Would you? I'd appreciate it. They're the lilac
leather cases!" she called.

Spur hurried out to the burned buildings, found
the two small suitcases and ran back into the trees.

She smiled as he placed the bags at her feet.
"Thanks. Aren't you the gentleman!"

He smiled and solemnly turned around, folding
his arms over his chest. "It's okay, Miss Thomas.
You can change now. I assure you I won't look."

She laughed. "Heck, call me Bev! And why
should I mind if you looked? You practically saved
my life!"

He stood stoically. The woman's proximity
reminded him of his own condition—he must stink

to high heaven. "How much water's up ahead, Bev?" Cloth rustled behind him.

"Lots. There's a spring and a big pool. The water's cold but it sure is refreshing."

He nodded. "Think I'll have a bath."

"Okay." She sighed. "I guess I won't have an audience after all."

He grunted and moved ahead to find the spring.

A dozen shades of green surrounded the six-foot pool of glistening water. The endless flow from deep within the parched earth had carved a large, deep bowl. Spur bent over it, cupped up some water and sucked it into his mouth. It was cold all right, he thought, and savored it as it travelled down to his stomach.

He ripped off his salt-caked clothing and threw it onto the ground. Sitting on the leaf-covered bank Spur tussled out of his boots and socks, stood and poked a toe into the water. Maybe too cold, he thought. Its temperature numbed his foot.

What the hell. Spur whooped, jumped up and splashed down into the spring. The water slipped around him like ice, jarring his body with intense pain and knocking away his breath. He gasped and hopped from one foot to the other as the water lapped at his waist. His whole body screamed in agony as he waited until it had adjusted to the sudden, glorious temperature change.

The sound of feet rustling through dead leaves behind him made McCoy spin around.

"I do declare!"

He glanced up, surprised.

Beverly Thomas, dressed only in her bloomers and silky chemise, locked her gaze on the long slab of flesh that swung between Spur's legs.

She sucked in her breath and smiled. "Aren't you a sight for a girl's sore eyes!"

7

Spur McCoy grinned up at Beverly Thomas as she stood gazing at him. He felt the heat of her eyes as she drank in his naked body.

"I thought you were changing," he said, somewhat uncomfortable. He shivered as a tiny wave of ice-cold water hit the small of his back.

Bev smoothed her hands over her chemise. "And miss all this—all of you—all of *that*? Not as long as I'm alive. I never miss an opportunity to see a buck-naked man." She pouted. "You probably think I'm a fallen woman, watching you like a dog in heat."

"Well," Spur said, noticing the swelling of her breasts beneath the flimsy chemise, "you've been through a lot. You're still in shock."

"The hell I am!" Bev smiled smugly at him. "Boy, you're just what I needed to make me forget my troubles." Her eyes sparkled at him for a moment before she dropped her gaze again.

Spur felt like a cow at auction as the beautiful woman studied his crotch.

"Mr. Burch, you've got more between your legs than the last three men I've been with put together!"

"I appreciate that, Beverly."

She jumped into the pool beside him. The resulting splash sent him into another shivering fit. Bev yelled in delight, rubbed her face clean, then arched her back before him, holding her arms high above her blonde-tressed head.

The woman's clinging, wet chemise revealed every detail of the pert mounds that lay beneath them. Spur forgot the cold water as he drank in her breasts—perfect globes that proudly jutted out from her body. They were topped with hard, red nipples that plainly showed beneath the wet silk.

Beverly finished her stretch and fixed her aquamarine eyes on his. "Look, Burch, I never was a woman who waited to be asked. I want you. Right now! To hell with the stage stop, to hell with Trevor, to hell with all that's right in this world! Frank Burch, love me!"

"I never say no to a lady." Spur felt the flush of warmth at his groin.

"Haven't I made it clear by now that I'm not a lady?" She curled her upper lip, batted her eyelashes and parted her lips. With a blissful sigh Beverly threw her head back and melted against him.

Spur gripped the woman's slender waist and, crushing her slick body to his, peppered her face with kisses. He murmured against her throat, then lifted his lips to hers. They met in a long, lingering, tongue-thrashing kiss. Spur felt his erection pounding against her stomach in spite of the cold water that splashed between them.

He broke the kiss. Beverly stared up at him with her honest, enflamed eyes. "Undress me. Now!"

Excited by her lust, McCoy gripped the chemise and slid it up off her body as she held her arms above her head. He pushed his mouth onto her left breast, touched his tongue to the hard, red nipple, then pushed it into his mouth.

"Mmmmmm. I like that." Her voice was husky with sexual passion.

Spur sucked the nipple, flicking his tongue over the hard nub. She moaned as he gently ran his teeth back and forth.

"Why, what is this thing?"

He lifted his head. "Hmmmmm?" he asked.

"This thing here!" She was teasing him.

His erection floated on the water between them. "You know damn well what that thing is!" he said, his desire growing stronger and stronger. The woman radiated sex. Her half-nude body seemed to heat the water by its mere presence.

"I just hope you know how to use it."

Beverly gripped his penis and stroked it tenderly. "My goodness, Frank honey, I've never seen anything like this. I mean, one this big!"

He squirmed as her delicate fingers pulled and prodded. The erotic pressure sent bolts of fire through his veins. She increased the pressure and speed of her strokes, groaning and marveling at the massiveness in her hand.

Spur quickly brushed it away. "You keep that up and I won't have a chance to use it."

Beverly smirked. "Okay. Let's get out of this danged water and get down to business!"

They lay on the mossy bank, entertwined like jungle vines. Spur ripped off her bloomers, cursing as they entangled on her feet. Beverly giggled.

"Don't you want me?" she asked as he rolled her onto her back.

Spur grunted. The blonde fuzz between her legs beckoned to him with a siren's song. He moved above her and, lifting himself on his hands and the balls of his feet, hung in mid-air. His penis nudged her pubic hair.

"I want you and I'm gonna have you!" Everything about the woman stimulated him, made him harder and ready to go.

Beverly stopped giggling and opened her eyes wide. "What kind of a lady do you think I am?" she asked, with mock indignation.

"You're not a lady. You're a woman. A woman in heat. A woman that's got me in heat." He positioned himself between her legs. Beverly lifted her hips in anticipation as he rubbed his erection against her opening.

He pushed. Hard. Beverly's mouth opened. Her eyes went glassy and she arched her back as he slipped into her, filling her with his desire.

Spur slowly pushed into a world of warm, moist velvet, opening her, pleasuring her. When he was in all the way he sighed and released the breath he'd been holding.

Their bodies joined at their crotches, Spur looked down into the aquamarine eyes of the woman who'd seduced him. The artifice, the teasing, the coquettry was gone, washed clean by the fire of pure erotic passion.

"Oh . . . oh . . . you're such a big man!" Beverly grasped his shoulders and pulled his body down onto hers.

"Am I too heavy for you?" Spur asked, nuzzling her right ear.

"You're not too anything for me," the breathy woman said. "But hold it there for a bit," she said, as his hairy chest crushed her breasts. "It's been . . . a . . . while."

He did so, unwillingly, but after enjoying their motionless connection for a few moments Spur felt the old urge building within him. He reared back and thrust.

"Yes!"

Again.

"Oh yes!" Beverly chewed on his stubble-covered chin and groaned.

Spur McCoy began stroking her, slowly at first, enjoying the ripples of emotion that shot across the woman's face as she took his penis. Bev clutched him, digging her fingernails into his back as he increased the tempo.

"Oh Frank, fuck me. Fuck me! Make me your woman!"

Spur's passion rose at the woman's use of the word. Snarling down at her trembling face, at her sex-misted eyes, he pounded between her legs, driving into her with sensual fury, luxuriating in the sensations their bodies were producing.

"Fuck me!"

Beverly lifted her thighs and locked them around Spur's. She came alive, bucking her hips upward, meeting his thrusts with her own, trying to drive him even deeper into her body. She reached around him and flicked her fingers across his bouncing, slapping testicles.

"Beverly, you feel good!" Spur said, his voice hoarse. He pumped into her faster and faster. "You feel so damn good!"

"So . . . so . . . do . . ." Her short, hard breaths blasted against his face.

He slammed his mouth down on hers, driving his tongue into her mouth, matching his thrusts into her vagina. She moaned and sucked it as their lips molded together.

He broke the kiss. Beverly's head flopped back as she frantically bucked her groin against his.

Spur lifted himself on his hands and stared down at the woman in wonder, in lust, watching her creamy white breasts bounce and shake as he opened her wider than she'd ever been before.

"Oh Frank, I'm gonna . . ." she began, panting.

"I think I'm gonna . . ."

Spur drove deeper, harder into her yielding opening until his hips became a blur. His vision blurred as wave after wave of pleasure shot through him. He groaned, driving them both toward that final moment.

"I'm gonna!" Beverly said, gasping.

He slammed into her with the violence of passion, celebrating her womanhood, reveling in his maleness. Spur's sweat rained down, splashing against her naked body like a summer thunderstorm.

Lightning struck her. Beverly moaned, gasped, closed her eyes and flipped them open. A high-pitched scream issued from her throat, followed by another and yet another. The woman's face flushed and grew slick as she shuddered through orgasm after orgasm, rubbing her clitoris against his erection, gripping his pumping thighs with hers as if to beg him to continue, to ride her forever.

Beverly's contractions, her cries of pleasure, her shuddering body drove him on and on. His mind went blank. His hips jerked spastically as he rammed into her, smashing their pelvic bones together.

Beverly gripped his hips and urged them faster. Spur felt his balls tightening in their sack as they banged against her buttocks. He felt his chest heaving, the pressure in his groin growing beyond denial. His vision blacked out. McCoy looked at the sky, screamed his primitive male cry of release and spurted deep within her.

Withdraw. Thrust. Spurt. He roared and shook and blindly slammed into her, ejaculating like a wild animal with no thought but for their mutual pleasure.

As she took his seed, Beverly shook through yet

another orgasm, clamping her legs around his spasming body, screaming and tearing at her hair as she shuddered through another mind-bending moment of pure sexual bliss.

After an endless time, it was over. Spur dropped down onto the woman. Their heated, slick bodies trembled as they maintained their union.

Slowly, slowly, Spur returned to normal consciousness. He felt Beverly's thighs relax and slip down from where she'd held them around his. With a great effort he lifted his head to look at the woman.

Beverly stared at him, astonished, her lips a dry, red bow. Her oval-shaped face glowed with satisfaction and her eyes narrowed as his penis jerked inside her. She squeezed her legs together around him.

"Anything wrong?" he asked, amused.

"No. I'm just surprised. I—I've never had it happen more than one time!" she stammered. "Never! Not even with the best! Jesus, Frank! You're amazing!" Beverly Thomas' voice was filled with wonder.

Spur smiled. "You're one hell of a lady—I mean woman, Bev." He tenderly kissed her lips.

"And you're a man and a half." Beverly pushed her hand down between them, past his hard stomach, and ran her fingers through his pubic hair. Spur groaned as she gripped the base of his erection. "You're still hard!"

He shrugged comically at her. "I guess it's the company." He started to withdraw.

"Don't take it out." Her voice was a whisper. "Don't ever take it out!"

He did, finally, a half hour later, after he brought them both to another shivering release. Spur rolled off the blonde woman and lay on the sandy bank of the spring-fed pool. They stared at the interlacing cottonwood trees overhead and, beyond them, at the deep blue afternoon sky. Beverly grabbed his hand and held it tightly.

"Jesus, Frank, after that I feel like I can face anything." She sighed deliciously and nestled her head against his shoulder. "I guess it's time to leave."

"Maybe you're right," Spur said. "Though I kinda hate to think about it."

She smiled. "Come on; we have to leave sometime. Besides, there's lots of time for more loving—later on. We'd better get dressed, get on your horse and ride out of here."

Horse. Spur frowned. How could he break it to the woman? "We can't."

Beverly looked at him, curiously. "What do you mean?"

He stalled. "We can't leave now. It's too late in the day to go very far before dark."

"Well, I don't mind riding after dark!" Beverly pushed herself up on her elbows and looked at him. "Besides, it'll be sexy with you pushing your thigh against my rump." Her eyes sparkled. "I may not know much about riding, but I'm a fast learner."

"We won't be riding." Spur sighed as the full brunt of their dangerous situation flooded back through him. They were in the middle of a harsh desert, miles from other humans. "I—I don't know how to tell you this, Beverly, but I don't have a horse." He looked squarely at her.

She smiled. "What are you talking about? Come on, don't tease me about a thing like that, Frank! Of course you have a horse!"

"No, I don't," Spur said sullenly.

She shook her head slowly, her eyes narrowing. The aquamarine circles seemed to pale. "You didn't ride up here then?"

"No. I walked."

Beverly laughed nervously. "Come on, Frank! You expect me to believe that you walked all the way across the desert? Well, I don't believe you!"

"It's the truth. Look. I took the Butterfield out from Clover. About halfway here we got attacked. The stage coach was wrecked, the driver killed, the horses put out of commission. So I walked about six or eight miles to reach this place. I don't have a horse, Beverly. That's the truth."

Beverly caught her breath. Her high cheekbones colored. "Attacked? You—you mean?"

He nodded. "Indians. Came out of nowhere. Killed two other men besides the driver."

She shivered. Anguish slipped over her face. "Well . . . what're we going to do?" she asked, squeezing his hand so hard that it hurt. "I mean, how are we gonna get out of here?"

"I wish I knew, Beverly. I wish I knew."

8

Spur pulled on his shorts and pants, stuffed his feet into his dirty socks and boots, slapped his Stetson onto his head and went back to the ruined stage stop. The bloated, dead horses reeked after baking in the sun as he passed them and walked into the charred building.

Sunlight glanced into it here and there where flame had licked holes in the timbers. Beside the overturned stove McCoy found a cache of canned goods. Most had burst from the intense heat, spewing their multi-colored contents onto each other, but he found a can of tomatoes and one of peaches that were still sound.

Poking around further revealed an untouched can of Arbuckle coffee, as well as a pot in which to brew it and two cracked metal cups. He also found a mass of sun-dried jerky and a barely singed loaf of bread no more than a few days old.

He went outside with the supplies. Two faded red blankets had been lain over bushes in back of the building to dry. Spur placed the goods onto them and wrapped them up, retrieved his saddle and carpetbag and headed back into the cotton-woods.

He and Beverly had spoken about their plans. They'd spend the night in the woods as Spur kept watch, then start for the next town a few hours before dawn to take advantage of the cooler night air.

As he arrived at the spring-fed pool Beverly Thomas was dressed in a bright yellow, high-waisted dress that she'd taken out of her travelling bags. She pulled and tugged the cotton material into place around her luscious body.

"Food?" she asked as he approached her. Bev was once again her vivacious self. She seemed to have shoved all thoughts of their dangerous predicament into the depths of her pretty little head.

"Food," Spur said, smiling. "Not much, but at least we can eat."

The blonde smiled. "Great! It seems like years since I've eaten anything."

Spur built a fire of the plentiful dead wood around them. The two ate in silence, alternately locking their gazes together and then letting the visual contact end. Spur pushed a fragment of the hard bread into the bright red tomato juice and ate the refreshing liquid.

Afterward, Spur poured the last of the coffee into the two metal cups he'd found in the burned building and they finished off the jerky and peaches.

"How long until dark?" Beverly asked as she delicately wiped the corners of her mouth.

"Not long. About an hour or so."

"And then tomorrow we'll walk to the next town. I don't know about that part. I never was the most active girl."

"You're active all right." He squeezed her left breast. "Active enough."

She giggled. "Frank Burch! That's not what I meant and you know it."

Spur released her orb. "We don't have a choice. We'll make it. You'll see."

"I guess we'll have to."

"Still think coming out here was a bad idea?"

She paused and then firmly shook her head, tossing her yellow hair around her like a halo. "How could I think that? I couldn't stay in Boston. Everyone there was so *stuffy*. That's no place for a girl like me to live. So in spite of everything that's happened, I'm glad I came. Besides, if I hadn't, I never would have met you."

"Thanks," he said.

"It's not every day a girl meets a man who can pleasure her the way you can." She smiled fondly at the memory, set down her coffee cup and lazily yawned. "All this loving and all this food's made me tired. I think I'll take a nap." She pulled a faded red blanket around her as she settled down on the soft sandy bank.

They rested until dusk. Spur woke and kept watch as the moon crawled overhead across the sky. The fire had burned down to glowing embers. He studied the moving pictures which the lines of red and orange created within them to keep awake. The steady, soothing trickle from the spring kept him company.

As Beverly slept all he could think about was the San Francisco mint and his saddle.

A lone rider walked his exhausted horse up to a ruined building. The thin moonlight was sufficient for him to survey the area.

"Hell!"

The tall man spat on the ground as he saw the overturned trough and the charred bodies eerily lit by moonlight that lay scattered around the place.

No water here, he mused. He'd just have to push

his horse farther. He surveyed the surroundings. Might be a stream nearby, he thought, looking at the dark shapes that jutted from the stark landscape not far from where he stood.

The man slid from his saddle and walked the protesting, lathered horse to the trees. He tied its lead to a sapling and walked a few feet into the grove. The darkness surrounded him, closing in on both sides where the branches choked out the glow of the moon. His boots crunched sand and dried twigs.

He paused in his tracks. A thin eddy of breeze trickled through the cottonwoods, sending their thin leaves whispering to each other.

It was nearly pitch-black. He shook his head. Maybe there was water ahead, somewhere in the woods, but he wasn't going to waste more time. His horse could make it. He'd give her the rest of the water in his canteen and go thirsty.

He returned to his mount and rode the bay toward the west, toward the next town and—he hoped—the start of his new life of wealth and leisure.

Spur poured sand over the dead fire and sighed. The last thing he needed on his mission was a beautiful woman to protect. But he figured he could take her to the next nearest big town— Yuma, he assumed—and then get on toward San Francisco.

Not that he minded. Meeting her had been the high point of his trip so far.

A distinct crackling sound broke the stillness surrounding him. Spur froze, listening. Six more crunches echoed through the woods, halted, then trailed away.

Someone—or something—was there in the

woods. He glanced down at Beverly. The beautiful woman was sound asleep, lying on her side, her arms pressed close to her breasts. Shallow puffs of air slipped through her lips. She'd be fine until he got back.

McCoy rose and moved like an Indian among the trees, soundlessly, without wasted motion. He walked among the cottonwoods for two yards, following the retreating footsteps, before he heard the unmistakable whinney of a horse and, seconds later, its hooves hitting the hard desert floor.

A horse! He ran out from the grove, no longer caring if he could be heard, and burst out from the trees just in time to see the diminishing figure of a rider rounding a nearby ridge west of the stage stop.

Friend or foe, help or threat, the man was long gone. Spur sighed and quietly returned to the spring, unsure whether he'd just spared himself further trouble or missed easy passage out of the desert.

Beverly was sitting up, stretching, as he walked up. "Something wrong?" she asked dramatically.

"No, nothing. I was just looking around." There'd be time to tell her tomorrow what had happened. She needed her sleep.

"Okay." She laid back on the blanket and dropped off again.

Spur frowned as he watched her sleep. In spite of his fortune in meeting Beverly Thomas, this hadn't been the luckiest day of his life.

Long before dawn tinted the eastern sky, McCoy and Beverly packed up their belongings and started on the long trip to Clover. They moved slowly across the silent desert, their passage unnoticed save for a pair of curious owls who hooted back and forth to each other.

Despite her earlier protests, Beverly proved herself a good walker. She'd changed her high heels for sturdy flat soled shoes. Spur was pleased that he hadn't needed to stop for rest nearly as often as he thought might be necessary.

They'd brought as much water as they could, plus an additional can of peaches that Spur had found moments before their departure. The sweet syrup and fleshy fruits would taste especially refreshing once the sun had reached the peak of its intensity.

They walked on and on, ignoring their personal edges of exhaustion, pushing harder, blocking out the misery that their bodies telegraphed to their brains. Beverly panted. Spur swore. Together they made their way toward the town.

It was sundown before they reached the outskirts of Clover, Arizona Territory. Once a Mexican ranching settlement, it was ringed with ranchos. Beverly had been tempted to stop at one of them on the way in but Spur had convinced her to wait for more satisfying luxuries—like private beds and real food—in the town itself.

The tall, muscled man and blonde woman attracted little attention from the citizens, a mixture of Mexicans and Anglos, as they dragged themselves down the manure-laden main street. Spur saw a sign on a false front with just one word—hotel.

They quickly checked into rooms, both on the second floor on opposite sides of the hallway. After they'd washed their faces and changed their clothing they went down the steep stairs to the front desk. Spur quickly ordered food, telling the Welsh proprietor that they were hungry.

He shook his head, saying that supper wouldn't be served for an hour yet and there was no way he was going to open the dining room early. Frustrated, Spur handed him a ten dollar bill. On seeing the money the greasy man hustled his eldest son into the kitchen.

Soon Spur and Bev were devouring mountains of potatoes, barbecued ribs, tortillas and beans. They washed down the hearty if simple feast with gallons of strong black coffee, then returned to their rooms, satisfied, weary from their long trek.

He saw Beverly safely to her room, kissed her forehead and unlocked his door. As he walked in and turned on the kerosene lamp, Spur realized he'd been too tired to worry about his saddle. He was relieved to see that it was still there where he'd lain it, over the pillow on the narrow wooden bed. He threw his hat into the corner and stretched out on the mattress. Sleep, he thought. He needed sleep.

Even the thought of Beverly's sexual favors—she'd made a half-hearted offer after their meal—wasn't enough to keep him awake. He drifted off into a faraway land where a broad, wide bay glistened in sunlight; where fog surrounded gleaming white houses; and where a white marble building waited the double-eagle dies that he'd been guarding.

A piercing feminine scream rocked him out of his sleep. Shocked by sudden consciousness, dazed by the scream, he twisted over and crashed to the floor.

"Beverly!"

9

Spur stumbled out of his hotel room and into the hallway, wiping sleep-grit from his eyes. A woman had screamed. Was Beverly in trouble?

He nearly bumped into a large object directly in front of his door. McCoy lurched back, focused his eyes and saw a short, fat, black-bonneted old woman poking her head into the room across from his. The elderly woman yelled and repeatedly slapped her beaded purse against some unseen object within the room itself.

"Thief!" she hissed. "Robber! Tryin' to take advantage of an old lady! How dare you break into my room and steal my things, you criminal!"

A red faced, huffing thin man—dressed only in his underdrawers—warded off the blows. "Now look, ma'am, this here's my room! I ain't trying to steal nothing from you. You're just all mixed up like."

"Rapist! Criminal! Gun-slinger!" the woman rattled on. "Think you're above the law! I'll show you what you get when you try to hoodwink Amelia Barrett!"

"But ma'am!" the protesting man said.

Spur shook his head in a vain attempt to strip it of the liqueur of sleep. This was the woman he'd heard screaming, he thought dully. Beverly must be fine.

Still unsteady on his aching legs, McCoy stared at the floor and turned on his heel. He bumped into the hotel manager as he rushed up to the scene. The unexpected impact sent Spur reeling back and banging against the far wall.

"Mrs. Barrett, please!" the sweaty, nervous little Welshman said.

She turned on him. "Mr. Jones, thank the Lord you've come!" the elderly woman said, smiling as her heavy purse connected with the 'robber's' left shoulder.

"Mrs. Barrett, you're waking up half the town!" The manager wore a striped shirt that hung below his knees.

"I don't care." She halted her blows. "I came back from havin' a drink and this man was in my room! Probably trying to steal my jewels or waiting to—to *rape* me!" She spat the hated word.

"I wasn't—hell, this is my room, Jones! I don't know what's gotten into her!"

Jones shook his head. "He's quite right, Mrs. Barrett. You're on the other side of the hall."

Amelia Barrett opened her mouth in surprise, glanced at the number on the door, at the blushing male hotel guest, then at Mr. Jones. " I—" She heavily sighed. "I'm sorry." Her sweet smile deepened the wrinkles that covered her face. "I guess I made a mistake. I'm an old woman; I don't see very well."

"Yeah, I guess so," the battered man conceded. "But that don't give you the right to—"

"Now Mrs. Barrett," Jones said, cutting him off. "Why don't you go to your room and get a good night's sleep." Jones put his arm around her and steered her to the opposite door. "Let's just forget about this."

"I guess I should. I'm so sorry to cause you so much commotion." Amelia glanced down at the innkeeper's bare legs. "And to get you out of bed too."

"That's fine. Get a good night's rest." Jones glanced at Spur, curtly nodded and walked down the hallway, peppering his movement with soft curses.

McCoy watched it all in a daze, leaning against the wall in rumpled clothing, his reddish-brown hair tangled around his hatless head.

Amelia Barrett turned to Spur as the male hotel guest slammed his door shut. "My my, young man. You must think I'm an old fool. I don't know what got into me. Except maybe age." Her clear gray eyes fixed on Spur's. "I do declare. I *do* declare, young man. You're the 'xact image of my son Dale!"

Spur nodded groggily. "I'm . . . I'm happy for you." He started for his room.

"No, no, I mean it!" she said, catching his arm.

He wearily turned toward her. "Ma'am, I appreciate it, but I'm bone tired. If you'll excuse me." He groggily tipped an imaginary hat to her.

"Why, it's *remarkable* how much you look like him. If you were a little older there wouldn't be any difference a'tall! Not a'tall!" Her beady eyes shimmered in the dim light thrown by the kerosene wall sconces that lined the hotel hall.

Sleep, Spur thought. After forty-eight hours without it the last thing he needed was an old woman grabbing his arm. He thought of the bed that lay waiting for him—and his saddle.

"Tell me something about yourself!" Amelia said, as a smile rewrinkled her dry skin. "You remind me of him ever so and it's comforting to see you, to be reminded of him."

"I'm sorry. I gotta get my sleep."

"No!" She thought for a moment, then looked openly at him. "I need a drink, after that I definitely need a drink."

"Drink it in good health."

She gripped both his shoulders. "Young man, you don't mean to tell me that you'd let this old woman go to the saloon all alone, do you?"

Spur shook his head at her. "No," he said. "I mean yes. Hell, I don't know."

"I should think not! A fine upstanding man like you don't have any reason to let an old woman like me expose herself to all sorts of who-knows-what!"

"Frankly, ma'am, I don't have the time or the inclination. I need to get some sleep!" Spur felt anger rumble through his veins and, at the same time, felt foolish directing it toward a sweet-faced, gray-haired, old woman.

"Well then, do you—" She hesitated. "Do you think you could go to the saloon and get me a bottle of something?" She opened her beaded purse and retrieved a few dollars. "Anything that's got a kick to it?"

Spur sighed. If it meant he could get back into bed any sooner he'd agree. "Sure. Just let me get my hat." He went into his room, stuffed it onto his head, visually checked the saddle, went out and locked the door.

Amelia Barrett handed him the money. "I'll be in my room," she said sweetly. "Thank you ever so much, Dale!"

He smiled at the mistaken identity. "Okay."

McCoy walked to the saloon, cursing the woman with every step. If he hadn't checked on the scream he'd be asleep by then, but if it had been Beverly— no, he'd done the right thing.

Two blocks down he bought a small bottle of red
wine at the saloon. It was still early in the evening
and he passed several men and a few women on his
way back to the hotel. As he watched one young,
delicate thing sashaying by, his right foot pressed
into something soft and gooey. Spur looked down
—he'd stepped in a pile of horse droppings.

Scowling, he scraped off his boot and hurriedly
returned to the hotel. He walked down the hallway
—and saw the door to his room lying one-third
open.

He had closed and locked it. The last traces of
mist left his mind as he approached the opened
door. Soft kerosene light made a golden arc on the
well-rubbed wooden floor below it. McCoy slipped
his hand down to his holster and lifted the long-
barrelled Colt .45.

He kicked the door open.

"Oh!"

Spur dropped his aim as he saw the intruder—a
gray-haired woman wearing a bonnet. She
straightened up over his carpetbag. What the hell
was she doing in his room? And how did she get in?

"Young man, what do you think you're doing,
barging into an old woman's room like that?"
Amelia demanded, her face red with rage.

Spur didn't buy it. Something was up. "Get lost
again, Mrs. Barrett?" he asked sardonically.

The old woman faltered, looking like a naughty
boy who'd tipped over an outhouse, then opened
her mouth and let out a piercing scream.

"Shut up!" Spur said. He threw the wine onto
his bed, stormed over to her and shook her
shoulders. "That's not gonna work this time, Mrs.
Barrett!"

The scream trailed off.

"What're you doing here? You can't convince me

that you've accidentally stumbled into two locked rooms twice within an hour—no matter how bad the locks or your eyes are."

"But I—"

"No. Don't say anything, grannie! We're going to talk to Mr. Jones."

Amelia Barrett retrieved her beaded bag from the bed. "All right! Maybe he can keep all these wicked men like you out of my room!"

Spur closed and locked his door, then escorted her to the front desk and banged on the bell. Soon afterward, as he firmly held the woman, the beleaguered innkeeper appeared.

"What in tarnation is it this time?" the Welshman thundered, then stopped. "Mrs. Barrett!"

"I think this sweet-faced old lady's a slick thief. Far as I can figure she cases guests and then breaks into their rooms when she thinks they won't be inside."

Jones turned to Amelia. "That right, Mrs. Barrett?"

"No! Why that's the most absurd thing I've ever heard! He's just trying to—to—"

"To explain why you've been caught breaking into other guests' rooms twice tonight?" He turned to Jones. "I just found her in my room after she sent me out on a little chore." Spur frowned.

"That's a little hard to believe."

"Sure; that's why it has to be true. Who'd expect her of something like that?" Spur pointed out.

"Hmm. Come to think of it, a young couple on their way to Yuma did find some things missing in their room yesterday. They left this morning." He scratched his stubbly chin.

"How long has she been staying here?" McCoy eyed the woman, who stubbornly kept her mouth shut.

"A week now. Says she's resting up before heading on out west."

"Appears she's doing more than resting. You better go get the law, Jones."

The innkeeper looked up quickly at Spur, then nodded. "Be right back. Don't let her go anywheres." He ran off.

"Well, Mrs. Barrett—"

"I have no apologies!" she said, her chin firm. "An old woman has to make her own way in this man's world as best she can. So just shut yer trap, you young buck!"

Spur smiled at the old woman.

An hour later Jones, McCoy and the sheriff checked the woman's room. They found three travelling bags full of paper money, gold coins, jewelry, pocket watches and various other items that the woman had pilfered. It amounted to a small fortune.

"Lock her up, sheriff!" Jones said.

Spur dragged himself into his room, locked the door and soon was fast asleep.

In the morning, Spur met Beverly in the hallway. She looked radiant in the bright sunshine that filtered in through the windows at each end of the passageway.

"How you feeling this morning?" he asked, grunting in appreciation of the way her bright red dress hugged her curved bust and hips.

"Wonderful!" Bev's eyes glistened. She dropped her dirty lilac bags, raised up on her heels, threw her arms around him and kissed his lips.

"Good morning to you too," Spur said, as she ended the kiss and licked her lips.

"When do we leave?"

"We?" Spur asked.

"Yes! When do we leave this miserable desert

behind and get on toward the coast, to San Diego
and my cousin Trevor?''

Spur looked at her in silence. "Beverly, there's
something I have to tell you.''

Her smile faded. "What?'' Bev seemed perplexed.

"Not here. Come to my room.''

"Gladly!'' She hefted the bags and followed him
in.

Once there, Spur glanced at the saddle before
turning to her. "Sit down—on the bed.''

She did so happily and started unbuttoning her
dress. "I was hoping you were in the mood!'' The
blonde giggled.

"No, that's not what I had in mind—'' Spur said.
He struggled to keep his thoughts clear. "Please,
Beverly, just listen to me.''

She stopped fumbling and sat quietly, folding
her hands on her lap. "Okay, I'm listening.''

"Beverly, I just want to warn you that I don't
think it's a good idea for you to go with me to San
Diego.''

Her jaw fell open. "But why?''

"I can't tell you. It'd be dangerous for you to go
with me. That's about all I can say.''

She laughed. "Hell, what do you think it's been
like without you?''

"No, Beverly, you don't understand.''

She studied him. "What aren't you telling me?
You aren't some kind of bank robber or something,
are you?''

"No. Worse.''

She thought for a moment, a finger to her lips,
then shrugged. "Well, if you can't tell me then you
can't tell anyone. And you can't give me a good
reason for not going with you!'' Beverly studied
him. "Frank Burch, after what I've been through I

don't relish the thought of travelling alone—not through these lands."

"I realize that, and sympathize with you, but there's quite a bit about me that you don't know. First of all, my name's not Frank Burch."

She nodded. "I didn't think so. The way you said it—" She shook her head.

"My name's Spur McCoy." He paused. How much should he tell her to let her know of the danger she was exposing herself to? "I'm a sort of lawman. I work for the government."

She smiled slyly. "A lawman! First one I ever had—or who's had me. So why all this secrecy?"

"I'm working on an important mission. I can't tell you what it is, but it's so dangerous that I—" He lowered his eyes. "I don't think it's a good idea for you to go with me."

"Why don't you let me be the judge of that, Spur McCoy!" she tilted her chin. "I kinda like the sound of that. You sure spurred me the other day." Beverly sighed. "Okay, all right! When's the next stage for Flagstaff tear outa here?"

"Noon today."

"Fine. Then I'll be on it. If you happen to be on it too, well, I'll just pretend I don't know you." She molded her lips into a pout. "I'd *hate* to get in the way of your precious mission."

Before Spur could respond to her taunt the woman dissolved into giggles, sending her breasts rolling and bouncing beneath the crimson dress.

"Beverly Thomas, you stop that!" Spur said. "I'm warning you, girl!" Spur's defenses weakened as she continued to explode before him. She collapsed on the bed and laughed.

"Allright, Miss Thomas. I can't stop you from riding the same stagecoach. But just remember—I warned you."

Her laughter trailed off as she sat upright and stared at him. "I'll remember. Now why don't you live up to your name and spur me again? Who needs breakfast?"

He obliged.

Five hours later they'd boarded the stage. Its grizzled driver, Mack Reynolds, grumpily took their money and hauled their luggage onto the rack. "Might as well leave now," he said, as Spur let Beverly onto the stage first. "No other customers today. Ever'one got off here."

Spur sat beside Beverly. Their thighs pressed together and she slipped his hand in hers as the carriage bolted into life and shot out of town.

The blonde woman laid her hand on Spur's shoulder. "I want it to be like this forever," she said, and licked his neck. "I don't want you to leave me."

Spur shivered as he felt the liquidy sensation. "Just remember, girl, we're not travelling together!"

Six hours later they'd started into mountainous terrain. The trail to Flagstaff rose dramatically from the desert floor. As they bounced higher and higher along the shoulder of a sweeping mountain Beverly clung to Spur. Her left hand slipped between his legs and gripped his crotch.

"Mmmmm," she moaned.

"Ah, Beverly, the driver," Spur said, enjoying the feeling.

"Let him get his own woman!"

As he responded to her intimate touch Mack Reynolds yelled and reined in the horses, sending them to a shuddering, hesitating stop.

"Damn!" Spur said, as Beverly retrieved her hand. They'd ridden into a small, isolated, high-

altitude town. Poking his head out the small
window as he adjusted his groin Spur saw a
sign—they were in Flagstaff.

They hurried off the stage. "We stop here for the
night," Mack Reynolds said. "Be on the stage first
thing in the morning, right after sunrise." The
driver leaned forward and threw Spur's saddle on
the ground.

"Hey!" McCoy said, bending to grab it. "That's
valuable merchandise! Don't go throwing it
around, Reynolds!"

"I've waited a long time for this day, Spur
McCoy!" someone said behind him. The voice was
thick with Latin nuances.

Spur spun around. A short, stocky, long-haired
Mexican man stood five yards from him, legs
spread, feet planted on the ground, both hands
hovering over his twin holsters.

"I've waited a long time to watch you die,
gringo!"

10

"Have we met?" Spur asked the puny Mexican gunslinger as they faced each other off in the streets of Flagstaff.

"You know we have! You killed my men. Tucson, a few years ago. I watch them die when you shot them. Remember, gringo? Remember how you killed?"

Spur shook his head and dropped his saddle. "Never been to Tucson. You must have me mistaken for someone else."

He did recognize the man—Roberto Costa, a notorious, small-time crook who robbed banks and held up stage coaches. His face was plastered on walls throughout the west.

"Why, his name's not McCoy!" Beverly said, walking up beside him. "It's Burch. Frank Burch."

"Beverly, go away," Spur warned.

"*Si*, pretty lady. Wait for me in hotel room." Costa sneered at her.

"But—"

"Go!" Spur shouted.

Frowning, Beverly moved to the other side of the stagecoach and glanced up at Mack Reynolds, who rubbed his hands together in apparent delight at the excitement.

"I don't know who you are or what you want, but

93

I'd suggest you get the hell outa here before you go and get yourself hurt." He held his own hand over the holster strapped to his thigh.

The small Mexican laughed throatily. "You scare me," he said. "I shake in my boots."

Spur stared the man down. "I guess you do. Look, Costa—"

"Ah! You remember?" he asked.

"Yeah, I remember. I couldn't forget your ugly face if I tried. You're wanted for bank robbery, extortion, murder, rape, and horse-stealing!"

The Mexican crook frowned. "I never steal horse! You lie! I buy horse."

"There's a $5,000 reward on your puny little head, Costa. Every lawman in the area knows that. You're damn stupid to show your face to me again."

Costa grinned. "I have friends here. I get protection. I was not planning, just saw you. So watch your back, McCoy. You not leave Flagstaff alive!"

"And you won't leave Flagstaff at all." Spur took a step forward. "Just come with me to the sheriff's office, Costa. Your riding days are over."

Costa laughed. "No, lawman! No fuckeen way!"

"Shoot him!" someone nearby said. "Shoot the old snake!"

"Yeah, Costa, blow his brains out!"

"Yeah, prove how good a shot you are!"

Saddened by the show of humanity around him, Spur scowled. If he drew, he'd force the man's hand. Too many innocent bystanders around to shoot it out right there and then. Besides, he knew Costa was a lousy shot. Quick on his feet, but couldn't hit the side of a barn. That's why he had been so dependent on his men.

"Costa, you couldn't kill me if you tried. You'd miss if you pushed your six-guns to my gut and fired."

The man's face reddened. "What you say to me, gringo? You make insult?"

"You're the worst shot for a hundred miles, Costa! That's why you've been laying low here; you can't find any good men to ride with you. You're nothing without your backups; a coward, a knee-shaking, yellow-bellied coward!"

A dollop of spit oozed over the man's lips. "You —you are asking for it!"

"Go ahead and draw. I'm sure all your 'friends' here would love to see the ground soaking up your smelly blood!" Spur's hand danced over his holster, his fingers twitching.

"You talk big, McCoy. Too big. Now you no more talk." The short bank robber flipped up both shimmering silver-plated weapons and trained them on Spur's mid-section.

"Go ahead, asshole! Shoot! Do it in front of all these people you've been lying to! Let 'em see what a lousy shot you are! Waste your bullets in the street! Go ahead!" He folded his arms on his chest.

"No!" Beverly cried.

"Damn you, McCoy!"

"Yeah, shoot the big-mouthed bastard!" a wizened old cowboy said nearby.

"Go ahead, Costa; you've been talkin' big, do it!"

The man shook. His hands trembled as his gaze burned into Spur's.

"Coward!" McCoy barked. "Shoot me!"

"Please, Spur, I mean Frank, I mean—oh hell, don't do this!" Bev shouted.

Costa shook with rage. "You bastard!" His twin guns spoke.

Beverly screamed. Spur stood his ground. The slugs slammed into the dirt at his feet.

As the explosions died out the citizens of Flagstaff murmured to each other.

Roberto Costa stood panting, gasping, his eyes blank, as his streams of blue smoke drifted from the barrels.

Spur strode over to him and slammed his fist into the man's jaw. Costa jerked backward. The weapons flew from his hand as his chin split open, pouring out blood. The groaning Mexican hit the dust.

"You won't be robbing any more banks," Spur said. He glanced up, saw a man with a star pinned to his striped blue and white shirt. "You the law here?"

"Yeah!"

"He's all yours. That's Roberto Costa, wanted for three or four robberies. Big reward." He shot the man a glance. "But I guess you knew that, didn't you?"

The man arched his left eyebrow. "What can I say? Thanks!. I—I shoulda done somethin' about him before, but I—I—"

McCoy felt a warm body pressing up against his. Beverly looked up at him, relieved, her face flushed.

"You sure know how to show a girl a good time!" Bev said.

"Come on."

Four blocks down the street in Flagstaff, a tall, wiry man busily pumped away on a stained mattress. He stared down at the plump woman beneath him, at her bored eyes, her slack jaw, her half-hearted attempts to show passion and involvement in their activity.

"More," Joanna said. "Oh yes. I cannot stand it. More. You're killing me with that thing. Do it harder." The whore's voice was flat, hollow.

He grinned. "I'm not paying you to talk."

"Okay, so I won't talk." She stared at the ceiling, avoiding her customer's empassioned, almost frightening leer. "Hurry up, wouldja? I'm hungry."

"Okay, missy. It won't be long now."

Lawson Amory closed his eyes as he worked the woman over. The thought of his future wealth heightened his excitement. His hips moved faster, his strokes grew more powerful, until each thrust sent the woman's head banging against the wall behind the bed.

"Hey, watch it!" she said.

"Fuck you!" Lawson said.

"You are, big boy, you are!"

"You little cunt! Hell, if you were any good I'd buy you and take you home."

"Oh sure," Joanna said. "Talk big to me."

"You don't know a damn thing about me. You don't know who I am or what I'm doing."

"I know what you're doin'." The whore smiled, showing a broken front tooth.

He snorted. "Tomorrow I'll be the richest man in the whole territory. Maybe richer."

"Right, and I'm Betsy Ross." She flared her nostrils with a sigh.

"No, damnit!" Lawson slowed down, frustrated. Her talk had taken him away from the edge of release. He sighed as he moved within her. Okay. He'd do it again, just one more time. It was worth it—who'd listen to a fat Flagstaff whore? Besides, it was the only way he'd been able to shoot for the past three weeks.

So he told her everything. As he talked the fire

burned between his legs. Sweat slicked his body, his blood boiled as he related every move he'd made, the defeats, the triumphs, all the planning that had gone into his mission.

She took it in, bored, uncomprehending. He smiled as he told her of how he'd sell them to the hightest bidder, set himself up for life and kiss the U.S. Government goodbye forever.

The image of the woman below him blurred. He squeezed his eyes shut as he saw himself weighed down with gold, every pocket overflowing, gold in his hands, between his teeth, wallowing in it, nearly suffocating in it.

He slammed into the squealing woman and sealed his vision with the pure energy of raw sex.

Moments later, she pushed him off her. Lawson luxuriated in the feeling of release. Warning bells went off in his head—he'd showed his hand again, threatening his whole mission.

But one look at the dead-eyed whore satisfied the doubt. She was so stupid she probably didn't understand a word he's said.

He was safe for another day or so until the next whore.

Beverly Thomas and Spur McCoy sat down to dinner in the hotel dining room. Four others were there as well, nudging each other as they recognized the man who'd brought down the Mexican bandit in the street earlier that afternoon.

"I can't believe it!" Beverly said.

"I told you it was dangerous, hanging around with me." Spur sipped a cup of bitter coffee.

"Dangerous?" She laughed. "It's about as dangerous as collecting buttercups in a field in Boston on a summer's day! You know how to take care of yourself, Spur McCoy." She clasped his hand over the table. "Honestly, I can't think of when I've felt safer."

He smiled and shook his hand free to dig into his dinner.

"That man had two guns!" Beverly said, breathlessly. "Two! And you just stood there, begging him to shoot you!" Her light blue eyes were wide with admiration.

"That wasn't bravery," Spur said. "He really is a lousy shot. Let's just forget about it, okay?"

"Okay." Beverly made a visible effort to temper her enthusiasm.

They ate in silence, aware of the stares that the other diners darted at them—and of their whispers concerning the man who'd brought Roberto Costa down before their eyes.

Mack Reynolds, dusty from the stage coach, hurriedly undressed as the naked, dim-eyed saloon girl lay on her bed. Joanna watched him as he revealed his pitiful, white, fat body.

Another screw, another dollar, she thought idly.

"I want something extra," the stage coach driver said as he rustled out of his black pants.

"Like what?"

He shrugged. "I don't know. Surprise me."

The woman sat up. "How about some information?" Her mind raced as she formulated her words.

"Don't you talk fancy, girl!" Reynolds said, grinning. "Information? What kind of information?" He dropped his drawers.

She flinched at the sight of his ugly genitals. "Good information. Mister, you like to make money? I mean, real good money?"

"Yeah, I guess so, but I like to spend it too." He flipped her a silver dollar.

It landed on the bed beside her. Revulsion rose in

her throat as the smelly, smiling man sat beside
her. She flinched from the touch of his body. She
had to get out of this town, out of this business,
and into a good marriage. She just couldn't take it
any longer. Making some extra money that she
wouldn't report to her boss would be a good start.

"Mister, I got some news that you might be
interested in."

"What kind of news?" he asked, impatience
hurrying his words.

"Just the kind that could make you rich."

He guffawed. "C'mon, Joanna; how'd a girl like
you know something like that?" Reynolds cupped
her left breast.

She squirmed away from him and pressed her
back against the bed. She slid her legs firmly
together. "I hear things. Lots of things from my
men. And I heard something today." She shook
her head. "You wanna know what it was?"

Reynolds slid a calloused hand between her
thighs. "Sure, girlie. Tell me everything. Just
spread 'em wide-like."

"Five dollars and I tell you everything." She
caught his hand and, with forced playfulness,
threw it back at him.

"Hey, what is this?" Reynolds asked.

"It'll be worth it, believe me." Joanna inhaled
through her mouth to keep from sickening herself
smelling the man's acrid sweat.

"And then you'll let me have fun with you? If I
pay this extra money, I mean?"

She nodded. "Sure. You can fuck me every which
way."

He quickly got the money and held it out to her.
"This'd better be good, dolly, or I'll take it back
from you."

She tucked the six silver dollars beneath the

mattress and stretched out on the bed. The slob-
bering man eased himself down on top of her,
crushing Joanna with his weight.

"Tell me!" he said, growing aroused. "Tell me
my five dollar's worth!"

Joanna took a deep breath, closed her eyes and
repeated every word the tall man had told her
about the dies for the gold double-eagle coin that
were in town.

11

As Spur and Bev ate breakfast in the hotel's dining room, McCoy saw the stagecoach driver arguing with a young couple outside the window. They seemed to want to get on the stage but, apparently, he wouldn't let them on.

"It's time," Beverly said, wiping her lips with a lace handkerchief.

They'd already checked out, so the pair hauled their luggage—including Spur's saddle—out to where the stage was parked at the hotel's boardwalk. The two teams of horses looked fresh and eager to be off.

"Some kind of problem?" Spur asked as he handed his saddle and carpetbag to the driver.

"Who? You mean that young couple?" Mack Reynolds snorted. "Wanted to ride for free. I told them what they could do with their free ride!"

"Can't you hurry?" Beverly asked. "The faster we get to Yuma the closer I'll be to the coast."

Reynolds jumped onto the driver's seat and feigned a bow. "If you'll step in, ma'am, we'll be on our way."

Spur helped her inside and sat across from her on the seats. "Guess we're alone again," he said pensively.

"So? Isn't it wonderful? Us here alone and him

up there where he won't bother us."

Mack Reynolds yelled and snapped his whip. The horses burst into action as the coach sped out of town.

"Yes . . . I guess it's wonderful." He shook his head.

She smirked. "What's wrong now, Spur? I mean, Frank?"

He'd told her to use that name when they were in public. Although she didn't know why, she had agreed to the plan.

"We'll be going through Indian country again pretty soon. A couple more able-bodied men who can shoot wouldn't be too bad."

"You can take care of us. And me."

Spur shook off the doubt. "You? Beverly, I don't know a thing about you. I feel like we've known each other for years but we only met a few days ago. Where you from?"

The blonde unpinned her bonnet and sat it on the seat beside her. Her hair fell to her shoulders. "There! That's better!" She affected a British accent. "I was born in Dover, in merry old England." Switching to her normal voice, Beverly explained, "But I really don't remember it. My father had gone to England on business—he was a ship-builder—and my mother happened to have me there just before they came back to the States.

"Anyway, I grew up in Boston in a big, old, ugly brick house by the bay. I can't complain about my childhood, I had everything I wanted, including this little gold-colored rope. All I had to do was pull it and a maid would show up and do whatever I asked." She shut her eyes. "I grew up wearing French dresses, eating caviar and *pate fois gras* for breakfast, had more money than I knew how to spend—but I was unhappy."

Spur smiled. It was a familiar story, but he asked her why.

"I didn't have any friends." Her high prominent cheekbones colored. "We lived four miles from the nearest road, out on a point of land. On one side the waves crashed below us and, on the other, trees stretched out to the road." Her face turned bitter. "My mother and father never talked to me, never kissed me goodnight or tucked me in. My family consisted of maids, butlers, groundsmen and stable boys."

Spur was silent.

Beverly brightened. "But that was okay. I didn't like them—either of them, so I pretended they didn't exist. It worked out fine, since they did the same thing to me."

"Why'd you leave home?" Spur asked. "Did you get married?"

Her eyes danced. "Not exactly. Oh, they tried. They tried to force me into marrying for six years, but I hated every man they introduced me to. They were all stiff-necked millionaire's sons whose wallets were probably bigger than their . . . well, *you know.*"

Spur nodded.

"Anyway, not long ago father went out looking for me. He found me out back near the trees with the stableboy. My bloomers were around my knees and, for some reason, the young man wasn't wearing his pants." She smiled at the memory. "That was too much for my parents. They handed me a thousand dollars, made me pack my bags and sent me off."

She paused. "So I thought I'd look up my cousin Trevor in San Diego. And that's why I'm here."

"I see."

Spur tried to picture Bev in those expensive

trappings but couldn't. She'd been raised to be a lady but—as she herself had said—she was much more than that. She was a woman.

"Enough about me," Beverly said. "Tell me about you. Why all this secrecy? Why this phony name and all that?"

Spur glanced behind him. The coach's noise probably drowned out most of their words so that the driver couldn't hear. But no sense in risking matters any further. He took her hands and leaned to her.

"No!" she said. "Don't say it! Let me guess. You can't tell me now." She studied him for a few seconds, lips pursed. "Is it something about that Robert Caustic or something?"

Spur smiled. "Roberto Costa and, in a way, it is something to do with that."

Beverly frowned at him.

"Believe me, Bev, it's better that you don't know."

She threw her hands up in the air. "Okay! Okay! Don't tell me. I'll just sit here and twiddle my thumbs until we get to Yuma."

"It's also safer if you don't know."

"All right! I won't ask you again." Beverly tossed her head, ran a hand through her mane, then drummed ten polished fingernails on the hard seat on either side of her. "So you're a lawman."

Spur laughed.

"And you're on some kind of secret mission."

He stared at her, darting his pupils back and forth.

"And it's dangerous, and somehow it involves Mexican—what's the word?—*banditos* and San Diego. How close am I?" Her eyes shone in the slanting sunlight.

He remained silent.

"Well, it looks to me like you're just lazing around, travelling from town to town, not doing much of anything, except helping out poor women in distress and inviting people to shoot you—and walking across the desert."

Spur grinned, crossed his wrists, laid them on the back of the seat and leaned his head against them. Beverly was amusing; he was enjoying this.

"I don't think you are a lawman, Sp—I mean, Frank Burch! I think you're just a—a—damn; I don't know what the hell you are!" She looked at him, perplexed.

He laughed out loud, jumped to the seat beside her and kissed her cheek.

"What's that for?" she asked as he pulled his lips from her face.

"For not asking me again!"

Two hours later Spur's butt was aching from constantly pounding on the hard seat. The stage coach rattled over the rocky, mountainous countryside, passing tall peaks. Some, thousands of feet high, were frosted with unreal-looking snow that glistened in the altitude-weakened sun.

They passed through tall, stout pine trees as they slowly made their way from Flagstaff. The driver let the horses pick their way down, not forcing them.

The time seemed to crawl by, Spur thought. Beverly, clasping his hand, had fallen asleep on his shoulder. He watched her as she napped.

Spur had begun snoozing himself when the stage came to a complete stop a few minutes later. He woke with Beverly at the snap of the reins and the driver's harsh voice. Spur stuck his head out the window.

"Why're we stopping?" he asked.

Mack Reynolds looked down at him, grim faced.

"You better come on out here, mister, and look at this."

"What the hell is it?" he asked.

"Just get out here!"

Cursing under his breath Spur opened the door. As his torso jutted out from inside the stagecoach McCoy felt a powerful blow strike his head. He groaned in surprise and pain and staggered forward for two steps. The agony increased, filling his brain and smothering his consciousness. His vision went black. His knees buckled. He was out before he hit the ground.

"Come on, shitface! Wake up!"

Spur groaned. The dull ache in his head, the hard ground pressing against him and the taste of dust in his mouth all told him where he was.

He opened his eyes. The brightness intensified the pain. As he closed them, Spur was aware of more pain coming from his ankles and wrists.

A low growl forced him to open his eyes again. Three feet away a scrawny, open-mouthed mountain lion snarled at him, saliva dripping from his razor-sharp fangs.

Spur groaned and shook his head. He ignored the pain as he looked at the big cat. It had been tethered to a dead, thin sapling. It tensed the rope and looked hungrily at McCoy, licking its lips, its eyes unblinking.

Beverly gasped. "Spur, I thought you were—"

"Shut your mouth, woman!" Reynolds yelled.

Ignoring the mountain lion, Spur tried to ease the strain in his shoulders and thighs but soon realized he couldn't. Ropes bit into his wrists and booted feet. They'd been tied together near the small of his back, completely immobilizing him.

He was hog-tied! Spur fought the bonds, struggled against them, flopping around on his belly like a gasping fish, as the cat continued to growl.

He heard a laugh. McCoy looked up and saw Mack Reynolds, the stagecoach driver, standing over him. "Save yer strength," he said. "You're gonna need it for talking."

"Spur, don't tell him—"

Reynolds spun on one boot and slammed his opened palm against Beverly's cheek. She screamed and wilted against the stagecoach.

"You bastard!" she said, rubbing the bright red hand-imprint.

"You'll get worse if you don't keep your fuckin' mouth shut, bitch! Maybe I'll feed you to the cat first! Hell, I ain't the kinda man who'll hurt a pretty woman, but you just might change my mind!"

Beverly fumed at him, but was silent.

Spur looked up at Reynolds as he turned back toward him.

"Well, Mr. McCoy, all comfortable?"

"Yeah." He blocked out the pain that rolled around in his skull and boiled up in his gut. "Reminds me of a saloon girl in Dodge City. This was her specialty."

Reynolds roared with laughter. "Cats and ropes? Hell, I ain't no saloon girl," he needlessly said.

"No. You're lower'n that. What the hell are you doing, Reynolds? Having a little fun?"

He tussled against the bonds, sending them scraping against his wrists and the tops of his boots. Spur McCoy was helpless. How the hell was he going to get out of this one, especially with that starved mountain lion staring at him?

"Sure, I'm having fun." He glanced at Beverly and groped his crotch. "I'll have some more fun later."

"If you lay one hand on me I'll kill you!"

"Hoowhee! I like a girl with spunk! But right now I'm all business."

"You look all bullshit from where I am," Spur said.

"You mean on your belly, hog-tied, seconds away from getting eaten by that big cat?" the driver snorted. "If I was in your position I'd shut my yap and listen. That's all you can do, far as I figure."

"What do you want, Reynolds?"

The man squatted before Spur, his back to the lion, and gazed down at him. "I want the two double-eagle dies you're transporting to San Francisco," he said evenly. "The ones you've had since you left Denver. And I want them now!"

Spur sighed. Again? Not again! "Reynolds, you must have shit fer brains. Where in hell'd you get such a stupid idea like that?"

He smiled. "None of your damn business! Are you gonna tell me where you're keeping 'em or do I have to use this?" He yanked a Bowie knife from his boot, waved it menacingly around McCoy's face, then pressed it against his neck.

"Maybe I could cut off your arms and legs, one at a time, until you told me. Or maybe I could start with your ears or fingers. Just chop you up into little pieces. Make it easy for that cat to gobble you up."

Beverly screamed again.

"Shut your mouth or I'll start on you, girl!" Reynolds yelled without turning from Spur. "What'll it be, lawman?"

Spur smiled. He had a plan. "Okay. So what happens if I do tell you? I suppose you'll just let me and the girl go. Right? Just leave us here . . . alive . . . with that mountain lion."

The driver spread out his hands. "But of course.

I'm not a violent man." The sunlight glinted on the razor-sharp blade as he waved it in the air.

The cat growled.

"I don't believe you."

"You got no choice, mister. No choice!"

The stagecoach driver's words stabbed the air, sending a fine spray of spittle onto his face.

McCoy flinched, then nodded. "Okay. I'll tell you."

12

With his hands and feet lashed together behind his back, Spur glanced over at Beverly. She shook her head at him, urging him not to, her eyes wild. He smiled at the blonde.

"Okay, I'll tell you where I hid them," Spur repeated.

"About time, McCoy!" Reynolds thundered. "I already know they aren't in your carpetbag or in your pockets. Hell, I looked under your hat and took off your boots to look there, but didn't find them. And hell, I had to put 'em back on. Your feet stink. So where are they?"

Spur thought fast. "My boots."

"I just tole you I looked in your boots!" Reynolds screamed. "What're you trying to pull?"

"Did you look inside them?"

Reynolds scowled. "You want me to let that big cat chew on you for a while, McCoy? Don't talk shit. What the hell do you think I just said?"

"Did you look *inside* them?"

"Hell, boy, talk straight? I'm getting damned tired of this bullshit!" He knelt and pushed the big Bowie knife against Spur's neck again.

Beverly gasped as the steel blade drove into the soft tissue a fraction of an inch. A bright red droplet rolled down from the wound. The mountain lion sniffed the air and roared at the smell of fresh blood.

"Did you look inside the heels?" Spur asked.

Reynolds withdrew the knife and sat back. "What're you talking about?"

"The heels. My boot heels. Did you look inside them, or just inside my boots?"

Reynolds laughed. "Matter of fact, I didn't. Mighty fancy place to hide 'em, McCoy! I never would've found them there. Now you just hold still while I take a look." The driver moved over to Spur's feet. His big, calloused hands gripped the squares of black leather and tugged on them.

Spur gazed at the mountain lion as the man worked over his boots. "Nice kitty," he whispered.

"You better not be shittin' me, McCoy!"

"I ain't."

Spur glanced up at Beverly. She stood still, hugging herself, shaking her head.

After struggling with them for a few seconds Reynolds tore his hands from the boots. "How the hell do I get into those damned things? I don't see no cuts anywhere, no place where you plugged up a hole!"

"You gotta take them off," Spur said. "I pulled up the lining, dug holes in the soles and stuffed the dies in. Then I glued the lining back down so it wouldn't attract attention, just in case."

"You could have told me that in the first place!" Reynolds huffed. "I guess we'll just have to get these things off."

He tugged at Spur's boots, pulled on them, yanked as hard as he could, but they wouldn't budge. The rope he'd tied around them kept them firmly planted on his feet.

"Take it easy!" Spur said. "Christ, you wanna

rip my feet off?"

"Better me than that cat. Damn! They're not comin' off!"

Spur was silent as the man thought it out. Go ahead, he said in his mind. Go ahead and do it.

"Guess I have to untie 'em after all. Don't go and do anything stupid, asshole! That cat smells its dinner. Now that I know where you hid 'em, your life ain't worth shit to me."

"I won't do anything stupid," Spur said, pretending weariness.

Mack Reynolds worked quickly. First he cut the lead between Spur's bound wrists and feet. McCoy obediently let his feet and hands flop down. He felt the man's knife slice through the knotted rope around his boots, tearing away at the coarse fibers a few at a time, working the blade into the mass until the last strand popped open.

His feet were free.

"Hold still," Reynolds said.

Spur waited until the big hands pressed around his ankles. He sharply yanked his legs apart and sent both feet rocketing up to smash into Reynold's face.

"Shit!" the man said, as the hard leather soles broke his nose and split both lips.

His hands still bound behind his back, Spur scrambled up into a sitting position and drove his boots into the groaning driver's stomach. The Bowie dug into the ground as the big man toppled over, yelling, covering his torn face with his hands.

Jumping to his feet, Spur struggled against the ropes. They wouldn't break. Reynolds hadn't left him enough slack to wriggle out of them.

The driver stumbled up into a standing position directly in front of the now pacing mountain lion. Blood poured from his nose. Spur gritted his teeth, bent at the waist and charged at him. His head slammed into Reynold's stomach. The driver grabbed McCoy's shoulders just as he tipped over.

Spur wrenched himself free. The big hands slipped off. Mack Reynolds crashed down onto the dead tree that held the mountain lion and broke it in two, releasing the animal.

The enraged cat, surprised at its freedom, roared and jumped onto the stagecoach driver. Reynolds screamed as vicious teeth tore into his arm, slicing through veins and arteries, ripping apart the skin. The mountain lion's mouth turned red with blood. The big man tried to fight off the cat but its teeth held him close.

Spur stood watching for a second, then turned and searched for the knife. There it was.

"Beverly!" he yelled above the agonized screams of the lion's living human meal. "Beverly!" He shouted louder.

She turned to him, tears streaking her cheeks.

"Get the knife and cut me loose! Hurry!"

"But—" She pointed at the wrestling man and mountain lion.

"Do it!"

Blubbering, she retrieved the Bowie from the dirt.

"Come on, cut the rope!" Spur turned his back on her.

Bev worked quickly, her sobbing increasing as Mack Reynold's screams intensified.

Cat and human thrashed on the dirt as Spur finally felt the pressure vanish from around his wrists. He shrugged out of the rope fragments and grabbed Beverly's hands. "Let's get the hell out of here!"

"But that man—he's—"

Spur picked up his saddle where it had been

thrown on the ground and yanked the blonde toward the stagecoach. He threw it inside.

Mack Reynolds passed out as the mountain lion ripped off his left arm at the shoulder and gnawed contentedly on it. Pints of fresh blood oozed from his maw. Torn muscle tissue and arteries stuck between his reddened teeth.

"Come on!"

Spur pushed Beverly Thomas into the stage, slammed the door shut and hopped onto the driver's seat. The horses were skitterish, whinneying at the violence and blood. He slapped the reins and yelled. The two teams jolted forward into action, happy to tear away from the scene of carnage.

As they reached the rocky trail Spur stood and chanced a look behind him. He watched as five fingers slipped down the big cat's throat.

Hours later in a dusty Yuma hotel room they listened to mariachi music filtering up to them from the street below. Fresh from their baths, Spur sat slumped on the bed while Beverly nestled her head in his crotch and closed her eyes.

"I can still see it—all of it."

He kissed her head. "I know. I can too."

"It was so—so horrible, Spur. I mean, that lion *ate him alive!*"

"Just be thankful it wasn't us."

She shivered. He smelled roses in her hair.

They'd made it to the next stop and had explained to its proprietors most of what had happened. Not all of it, just that the driver had been killed by a mountain lion during a piss-stop. After digging into his funds, Spur had rented two horses and a saddle from the stage stop's proprietors.

They'd eaten, loaded up on provisions and water and then rode through the rest of the afternoon and night, finally reaching Yuma just before dawn.

Now, as they listened to the loud, cacophonous music of the roving Mexican band, Spur rubbed his lips against Beverly's.

"We've made it," he said.

She looked up him hopefully.

"This far."

Beverly was silent for a moment. "And what about tomorrow?"

"We'll have to wait that out."

During their long trip Beverly hadn't pressed him for details. She hadn't asked him about the double-eagle dies or anything else that the man had said. However, he did notice her glancing at his boots at odd moments.

Once, while they were riding side by side on the trail to Yuma before dark, she gazed at his right boot for several seconds, her eyes moving as it bobbed in the stirrup. When he'd caught her looking she shifted her gaze to the ground below his mount.

Spur figured that she either didn't want to know or didn't want to bring back the horror of the driver's death by asking him about it.

"I didn't put them in my boots," he said softly, still looking into her eyes, as they lay on the bed.

"You didn't put what—oh." She moistened her lips. "Where did you put them?"

He shrugged. "Guess. You're the lady detective."

Beverly frowned, then looked around the room. "That man said they weren't in your bags. If they aren't in your boots or in anything you have on—" She looked up at him triumphantly. "Your saddle. You put them in your saddle!"

McCoy smiled. "Very good, young woman, very good. You are an astute observer."

"Oh, thank you kindly, sir. And just what is my reward for being such an astute observer?"

Spur smiled. He recognized the fire in her eyes and realized there was only one way for Beverly Thomas to exorcise the terror she'd been through.

Though he was bone-tired, though his wrists were slashed with red rope-burns, the tiny hole on his neck stung and his back still ached from the uncomfortable position, he felt his excitement growing.

What the hell, he told himself. "You know what your reward's gonna be," he said, and smiled at her.

She slid to the floor and began tussling with her dress. "Close the curtains, will you, Spur? I think they can see in here from the building across the street."

Spur nodded and went to them. As he reached for the dust-caked, flimsy curtains his gaze zeroed in on the figure of a tall man walking down the street in the early morning light.

For some reason the face captured his interest. McCoy strained his eyes as the man approached the hotel.

Lawson Amory, Spur thought, when the face came into focus. Lawson Amory in Yuma!

"Spur, you coming back to me?" Beverly asked.

He shut the curtains and turned to the blonde woman. "Sure, honey."

"Anything wrong?"

"No. Just thought I saw someone I knew."

What was a Secret Service agent doing in this town? Why hadn't he been informed that Amory would be here? And why did Spur have this nagging feeling.

13

Lawson Amory walked down the dusty street, spitting trails of saliva. Spur McCoy should be in town by now, he mused, watching the men who passed him, searching for the now familiar mutton-chop sideburns and the brown hat ringed with Mexican coins.

Yuma was the last town in Arizona Territory before the border of California. Even in the early morning sun it baked with a dry heat. But it was alive.

Chickens scurried before a large Mexican woman who flailed her arms in a vain attempt to catch them. Drifters slept off their whiskeyed nights in the shadows that hugged adobe walls along the broad avenue. A boy of fifteen tagged behind a colorfully dressed—but far from talented—mariachi band as it blasted its way down the street, alternating music with vociferous announcements that somebody-or-other's cantina had just opened for business.

Amory saw no sign of the Secret Service agent but knew he would find the man. He always did. And this time—this time he'd get the dies from him.

Amory had known that it wouldn't be an easy task. He'd prepared as well as he could, for Spur

McCoy's ability to handle himself with his body and mind were legendary throughout the service. McCoy was held up as the surpreme example of what a good agent should be like.

As he wandered down the dusty street, sweat popping out on his neck, Lawson Amory felt energized. He was going up against the best. He was going for the biggest prize. He'd risked everything, given up everything for it.

And soon, after he'd tired of playing with the man, it would be his.

After his latest sexual romp, Spur trailed the chilling water over Beverly's left breast. Beverly squirmed as the white cloth pressed against her mound and droplets slid down her naked body to soak onto the towel below her.

"Too cold?" Spur asked as he dipped the cloth back into the flower-festooned ewer.

"No. It's delicious."

They bathed each other until the last traces of sweat and sex lay seething in the clouded water and the pitcher sat empty.

As he towelled Beverly, Spur thought back to what he knew about Lawson Amory. The man was an agent, that much was for sure, for they'd been introduced at some party during one of his infrequent trips back to Washington, D.C.

Amory was tall and wiry and an excellent shot. Spur seemed to remember hearing that he was skilled in Indian ways, knew how to move through heavy brush, could live off the land if he had to.

They'd been introduced—how long ago was it now? A year? Two? Spur couldn't remember. But the name, the man's craggy face and height had stuck in his mind.

Spur dug the towel between Beverly's round, full

white buttocks. She giggled as he moved it lower
and touched it to her lips.

The image of a shadowy face flashed through his
mind. McCoy yanked away the towel.

"Hey! Just when I was enjoying it!" Beverly
said, protesting.

When he didn't respond the bare blonde bent
over and looked at him between her shapely legs.
"You still there, Spur!"

"Yes. Just thinking."

She sighed and grabbed the towel. "If you're
gonna think let me do you now."

Spur was barely aware of her attention as he
remembered the face he'd seen—briefly—in the
darkened Little River hotel room. Amory? It could
be. Lawson Amory might have been the man who'd
broken into his room, stuck a revolver into
McCoy's mouth and threatened to pull the trigger.

It didn't make sense. Agents didn't go around
threatening each other. Unless . . . unless he had
been mistaken. Unless the man had gone crazy.

Or unless Lawson Amory no longer worked for
the U.S. Government.

"Mmmmmm." Beverly roughly stroked Spur's
hairy, muscled thighs and dabbed at the droplets
of water that clung to his pubic hairs.

He shook the confusion from his mind. No sense
in wasting energy just wondering. He'd better
send a telegram to the home office and find out
what the hell was going on.

The soft cloth moved lower. Spur smiled. " Dry
me some more there."

The towel flicked back and forth, up and down.

Perhaps Amory had heard about the movement
of the dies. He was certainly in a position to do so.
Maybe over drinks with one of the other pseudo
couriers he'd heard the news and had seen his

opportunity.

Maybe.

Spur smiled down at Beverly. "Let's get dressed. I have some things to do."

A half hour later Spur had sent a telegram to General Halleck in Washington. In it, in plain, simple language, he asked what Lawson Amory's current job was. Might as well end that avenue of thought quickly if the man was still in the service or if he was somewhere else in the country.

After all, he could be wrong about seeing Lawson there in Yuma and about identifying the man in his Little River hotel room as Amory.

Bevery had donned a bright yellow sun dress, with a matching bonnet and a small parasol. As they strolled down the boardwalk, dodging Mexicans as well as Anglos, Spur searched for the tall Secret Service man.

The smell of Yuma rose up around them. Onions, peppers, frying tortillas and beans, spicy pork and stale lard filled the air. The pungent aroma of horse droppings littering the street mixed with the more appetizing odors, causing Beverly to push a handkerchief over her face.

"I don't like this place," she said summarily behind the silk cloth. She surveyed the flat, barren land. "There's no trees, no flowers, only dust and dirt and sand and that horrible music."

Spur smiled. "Come on; it's not so bad when you compare it to where we were this morning. At least there's no mountain lion here."

She shivered. "Thanks for reminding me."

They approached a long, solid-looking building. "What's that?" Beverly asked.

"It's a great place to visit," Spur said with feigned excitement. "That's the Yuma Territorial Prison."

She pressed closer to him. "I knew I didn't like this place!"

He laughed as they passed it.

Soon they saw a crowd gathering on a corner up ahead and joined it. The object of their attention was a round-cheeked, sweating, bald-headed man holding up a mysterious blue-glassed bottle.

"Yes, ladies and gentlemen; the miracle cure of the 1800's! Professor Johnson's Liquid Elixir! Cures whatever ails you! Chills, infirmities, colds, weak hearts? Just take a spoonful of this magic philtre and be cured!"

"Does it grow hair on your head?" a cowboy asked.

The bald-pated snake oil man smirked. "That's the only thing it won't do, sir! Barrenness? Deformities of the limbs? Curvature of the spine? This'll do the trick! Professor Johnson's Liquid Elixir! Patented in the year of our Lord 1860! Good for whatever ails you! One thin dollar per bottle to cure your fatigue and fainting spells!"

"I'll take a bottle," a grizzled old-timer said. He proffered a dollar bill.

"Bless you, father," the salesman said, quickly exchanging bottle for money. "Potions and lotions and nostrums! Good for whatever ails you! Who'll be next?"

"What—what's he doing?" Beverly asked. She was fascinated by the man's tirade.

"Trying to make some drinking money," Spur said.

"I've never seen anything like this," Beverly said, her aquamarine eyes shining below her bonnet. "I think I'll get a bottle."

"No, Beverly, don't. You're just wasting your money. Trust me."

"Well, if nothing else it'll be a keepsake. And the

bottle's pretty too." She dug into her purse and handed a dollar bill to the drummer.

"Thank you, young lady," he said. "Good for women's sickness too."

Beverly grasped the thin bottle in her hands and removed the cork. She smelled it and wrinkled up her nose.

Spur smiled and surveyed the crowd. Across the street, near See's Livery Stables, Spur saw Lawson Amory glance at the crowd and dawdle aimlessly down the street.

Spur was certain the man hadn't seen him. He fought off the urge to follow Amory, unwilling to drag Beverly into the problem or to leave her alone on the street. Itching to confront the man, he glanced back at her.

Beverly held the opened bottle in her hands. "Might as well try it." Before Spur could stop her she put it to her lips and tilted it, swallowing half of its pinkish contents.

Beverly immediately pulled the bottle from her mouth, dropped it and retched. She pressed one hand against her chest and coughed, gagged, as the 'medicine' tortured her throat.

"You all right?"

The beautiful blonde woman paled and coughed, bending at the waist as her body tried to expel the liquid. She shook her head.

The crowd—and the drummer—turned to watch the choking woman.

"Hey, salesman, that's what your miracle cure does?" Spur escorted the gasping woman back to her hotel room.

Beverly stretched out on the bed in her sun-splashed room, fanning herself and sipping a glass of water.

"You all right?" Spur asked, turning over the

blue bottle in his hand.

"I'm fine now. I feel so foolish, being taken in by that—that—"

"Snake oil man." He frowned. "This curing elixir seems to be nothing but castor oil, grain alcohol, a dash of perfume and some kind of coloring." Spur glanced at her. "It could have been worse."

Beverly nodded. "I know. Thanks."

Two hours later, Spur felt all the coffee he'd drunk that morning threatening to split him in two. He excused himself and headed for the two-hole outhouse behind the hotel. He pushed the rickety door open and stepped inside, turned and shut it.

Spur grabbed his buckle. The door suddenly shot open. Surprised, McCoy looked up. Lawson Amory stood pointing a shotgun at his gut.

"We meet again, McCoy." Amory smiled.

"Yes, I guess we do, Amory. What the hell are you doing in Yuma? You on government business?"

Amory stepped into the doorway. "Not really. Just setting myself up for the future."

The barrel prodded Spur's stomach.

No time for talk. McCoy kicked the door. It jumped forward, groaned on its hinges and banged against the shotgun. Spur jumped as the big weapon exploded, peppering the door with lead.

"Bastard!" Amory yelled outside.

Standing on the seat, Spur yanked the door open and drove a foot into Amory's face. The tall man groaned and reeled backward, firing another load of buckshot into the air.

McCoy pounced on the man, knocked him to the rock-strewn ground and straddled his legs. He wrestled the weapon from the agent's hands and bashed the stock twice into Amory's forehead before the man gurgled and lay still.

Panting, Spur rose and stared down at the unconscious man. He hadn't been wrong. Lawson Amory wasn't on any assignment. He was in Yuma to steal the dies! Hell, he must've been following him from the day he left Denver.

McCoy didn't attract any attention as he hauled the man to the local sheriff's office.

"What's this?" Sheriff Oscar Tate said as Spur entered the small, squat building with Amory in tow.

"This man attacked me while I was tryin' to piss." Spur dumped Amory on the floor and wiped his gritty neck.

"And who the hell are you?" The thick-waisted man looked at Spur with narrow eyes. He ran a finger through his thick, prematurely-grey beard.

"Spur McCoy."

The man laughed. "Sure, and I'm President Grant."

"You've heard of me?"

"Of course I've heard of Spur McCoy—not you. Every lawman this side of the Mississippi's heard of McCoy. You got some kinda proof?"

Spur sighed and dug out the telegram he'd received from General Halleck detailing his latest job. He handed it to the doubting sheriff and looked down at the prone man.

Tate grunted. "Well, okay, suppose'n you are Spur McCoy—and I ain't saying you are. What the hell you want me to do with this man?"

"Keep him locked up. I don't know exactly what's going on here but I intend to find out. I sent a telegram to the home office in Washington; should get a reply soon. Maybe that'll clear up this whole matter."

Tate looked down. "You know who he is?" The sheriff planted his folded hands on his protruding belly.

"Lawson Amory. Do me a favor, sheriff; just keep him under lock and key until I get back."

Tate nodded. "Tell me more about this mission you're on."

Spur frowned. "I can't talk about it, Tate. And I'd rather you didn't tell folks around here who I was. Got that?"

"Sure, sure, sure. Okay, I'll corral him for now. What's the charge? Assault?"

"Attempted murder would do as well. He pulled a shotgun on me."

"Okay, okay, McCoy." Oscar Tate smiled amicably. "Good to have you in this hell-hole, if you really are who you say you are."

"Right." Spur grimaced and returned to his hotel room.

Three hours later, after playing ten hands of cards with a completely-recovered Beverly, he checked at the telegraph office.

"Just came in," the squinting clerk said. Leaning on a cane, he walked to a box stuffed with envelopes and rifled through them. "Here we go, sonny."

"Thanks." Spur walked out into the sunlight and read the message that the clerk had recorded in his barely legible scrawl.

LAWSON AMORY NO LONGER EM-
PLOYEE OF U.S. GOVERNMENT . . .
STOP . . . TERMINATED HIS EMPLOY-
MENT THREE WEEKS AGO . . . STOP . . .
NO WORD ON CURRENT WHERE-
ABOUTS . . . STOP . . . GOOD LUCK . . .
STOP.

It was signed General Wilton D. Halleck (retired).

Spur crumpled the yellow paper and stuffed it into his pocket. Amory wasn't a Secret Service Agent? It was time he talked to the man.

He dug his heels into the dirt and sped toward the sheriff's office.

Oscar Tate was stuffing a huge forkful of deep dish apple pie into his mouth. He waved at Spur and motioned to his busy mouth.

Nodding, Spur glanced at the two cells behind the man. Both were empty.

Blood pounding in his brain, McCoy slammed a fist onto Tate's desk.

"Where the hell's Lawson Amory? Where's the man I brought you just a few hours ago?" he demanded.

Tate swallowed and licked crumbs from his lips. "I let him go."

"You what?"

"I let him go! Hey, McCoy, anyone can make a mistake." He tongued apple goo from his teeth and gulped it down. "Seems the man you had me lock up was some kind of lawman too—the Secret Service, I think he called it." Tate shook his head. "Anyway, he showed me some kind of document that looked pretty damned convincing to me. He told me you're Spur McCoy all right and said you'd made a mistake. So I let him go."

"Damnit, Tate! You don't know what you've done!"

"The hell I don't!" The sheriff's face grew red.

Spur retrieved the crumpled telegram he'd just received and threw it at the sheriff. It landed on the pie.

"Get a mouthful of that!"

Grumbling, the corpulent man removed it from

his dessert, smoothed out the paper, read it and frowned. "So what's this mean?" The fat sheriff burped.

"Can't you read? Lawson Amory is no longer an agent. You let a renegade Secret Service man out of jail—a man who just tried to kill me. Jesus, Tate, you don't deserve to wear that star on your chest!"

"Like I said; anyone can make a mistake." He curled his upper lip. "But I don't care who you are, get the fuck outa my office!" Tate filled his mouth with more apple pie.

Spur grabbed the telegram and stormed from the place, his face reddened with rage. He cooled off as he neared the hotel. Served him right for trusting that slick-tongued man to a small-town sheriff.

So Amory was free again. The ex-Secret Service agent was somewhere in town, waiting for his next chance.

And Spur had better be ready for him.

14

In a dry wash five miles outside of Yuma, Lawson Amory rubbed his aching head and took another swallow of whiskey, then another. The alcohol soothed the dull throbbing in his forehead, tranquilized his bursting hatred, lulled him into a hazy, peaceful state.

Moments later he smiled in spite of himself, as he remembered how he'd woken in the cell, quickly collected his thoughts and outsmarted that stupid sheriff into setting him free.

As the wood-flavored liquid burned down into his stomach Amory tipped some water from his canteen into a small coffee pot and hung it from the crude tripod he'd constructed. As it brewed he settled back against the hard-packed sand wall and thought of how he'd come to be there.

He'd been born to a common whore in Philadelphia and left on the steps of an adoption agency at the age of two. Three years later a wealthy Philadelphia family, unable to have children of their own, adopted him and brought him into their world.

Lawson had grown up knowing he was an outsider, and his adopted father and mother had continually reminded him of how lucky he was to have been spared the torture of living in an adoption agency until his eighteenth birthday.

With his increasing years—including stints at private schools—Amory became less and less enchanted with his parents. When he was nineteen years old he'd balked at his father's offer to join the business—cash register and scale manufacture —and accepted a lucrative offer from one of the old man's major competitors.

Summarily disinherited by his family and bored at his new job, Amory joined up during the great war. He excelled in combat and enjoyed promotion after promotion. His father, intrigued by his son's advancement and the extra prestige it would give him in the yankee business world, pulled strings to get Lawson a lieutenant's commission.

Once the North had won and he'd entered civilian life, his father had again approached him to enter the family business. But again he'd snubbed the man.

Looking for a new career, Lawson Amory had joined the Secret Service shortly after it had been created to ferret out counterfeiters and to protect U.S. currency. During his army career he'd acquired a taste for danger and felt a rush of intense, undefineable excitement every time he faced another human being and blasted him into the next world.

However, Secret Service life wasn't what he'd thought it would be. Sure, there were times when he saw action, when he never knew if the next breath he took would be the last, but for twelve months he'd been doing nothing but sitting in Washington D.C. squiring around gold shipments and romancing senators' daughters.

He'd wasted his days and spent his nights locked between the thighs of plump women yearning for a real life, the kind that could only be won or lost by his skills at firearms.

During his years in the Secret Service he'd heard of the exploits of one Spur McCoy. The man was damn near famous for his ability to complete his assignments no matter how tough, impossible or dangerous they were.

A few weeks ago Harris, a new agent who'd been with the service for only a year, took him out for a drink to celebrate. Harris's new assignment, the greenhorn had told him, was to act as a decoy courier.

Amory hadn't been too interested until he heard who—and what—he was the decoy for. Dissatisfied with his life, thirsting for excitement, Amory saw his chance to live the moneyed life he'd once enjoyed, as well as the opportunity to pit himself against the foremost Secret Service agent.

He'd spent a week gently grilling Harris for details, then quit the service once he'd learned of Spur McCoy's plans and had mapped out his journey.

Somewhere between Denver and San Francisco he'd get the dies and settle down where the women were pretty, the whiskey was full-strength, and life was a mosaic of shootouts, spent shells and blood-soaked dirt.

A low hissing noise brought Amory back to the present. The water was boiling over the fire. Amory lifted the pot from the tripod and quickly set it on the sand. Soon, he told himself. Soon he'd be ready.

The dark-skinned man looked down and ripped the home-made knife from the uniformed guard's bleeding back. He pressed a shaking hand against the man's neck. No pulse.

Good. He was dead.

Glancing both ways, the prisoner bent and quickly stripped the guard. He had no more than two minutes. Once the dead man lay in his underwear, the Mexican tore off his drab clothing and dressed. The pants were too long, so he rolled them up. The shirt was far too big but he tucked in the tails and tried to smooth its billowing back against his body.

Working methodically, breathing evenly, the prisoner stuffed his feet into the black shoes and stood upright. He mentally checked himself, running his fingers over the buttons, making sure everything was in place.

It seemed right. He gripped the dead man's hat and put it on his head, then padded softly down the blank corridor. The door at the far end grew closer and, with it, his chances for freedom.

Ten more yards, the prisoner thought, as he moved in the uncomfortable, two sizes too big uniform.

"Hey! You there!" an American called as he passed an intersecting hallway.

The prisoner grunted and continued on.

"Hell, I'll tell you later."

The prisoner released his breath. Five more yards. Two. One.

He pushed the key into the lock. It hesitated, locked and turned the tumblers. He yanked it out and burst outside.

Free from the prison, the Mexican bolted down the darkened street. Few people were on the street; the stores were closed. The smell of tobacco and whiskey urged him into the first saloon he passed but the prisoner fought his desires. There were more important things to do.

He breathed heavily with excitement and fear.

He'd gotten out. He'd escaped! The bumbling
Americans had left him the perfect opportunity
and he'd taken it. All he had to do was get out of
town. Somehow.

A familiar uniform approached him a block up
the street. The prisoner panicked and bolted down
a dark alley. Think, his mind screamed. A narrow
stairway led to the second floor of the back of some
building.

The Mexican went up it, three steps at a time,
and tried the knob at the top. The door opened. He
slipped inside and pressed his back against the
wall.

A hotel. He was in a hotel corridor. The Mexican
smiled. He'd need regular clothes anyway. He
stuffed his hands into his pockets and once again
retrieved the small ring of skeleton keys. It was
worth a try.

Footsteps resounded from below. Someone was
coming up the stairs. He ran three steps to the
door opposite him and stuffed a key into the lock.
It wouldn't budge. Frantic, he fumbled with the
ring, found another key and pushed it into the hole.

It turned. The knob opened under his sweating
hands. Inside, he slammed the door shut. The
kerosene lamp was low but he saw the carpetbag
on the bed and the saddle on the pillow.

Hurry, he urged himself. Change and get the hell
out of there. Before they put you back into the
living hell that is the Yuma Territorial Prison!

"Honestly, I can't wait to see the blue waters of
the Pacific Ocean." Beverly sipped a glass of milk
as they ate in the hotel dining room.

"It's not much different from the Atlantic,"
Spur observed. "Just another ocean."

"Oh Frank, you're such a romantic," the woman

deadpanned. "I don't care. It's so—far away, so mysterious." She smiled and wiped her lip with a napkin. "California!" Her voice was breathless. "Flower-draped *ranchos*. White missions shimmering in sunlight. The smell of golden poppies."

"That's not why you're going there."

She pursed her lips. "No. You're right. But I can dream about it anyway, can't I?"

Spur shrugged. "Sure. Until you realize it's an untamed, harsh, barely civilized frontier."

"It can't be any worse than this place."

"I won't argue with you there. San Francisco's a big town but San Diego's just a fishing village with a mission."

"My cousin Trevor said he's doing quite nicely in that 'fishing village,' buying and selling land."

"We'll see once you get there." He pushed away his plate and stifled a burp. "Boy, that was one good dinner."

Beverly's eyes sparkled. She leaned closer to him. "Would you like dessert—in your room upstairs?"

He squirmed as the whisper tickled his ear. The woman was insatiable. "Sure."

She gripped his hand as they climbed the stairs. "How long until we get to San Diego?"

"Two, three days at most."

"And then you'll be going to San Francisco?" Beverly asked as they reached the landing.

"That's right."

"Hmmmmmm."

Spur stopped them in front of his door. He pushed the key into the lock but the door opened.

"Stay back, Bev." Spur banged the door open.

The room was empty, the lamp still low. He turned up the flame.

"Everything okay?" Beverly asked as he walked in.

Spur hesitated. His carpetbag had been overturned. His belongings were scattered across the polished wooden floor. Spur's gaze darted to the bed. The pillow was creased with deep impressions —and his saddle was gone.

"No, it isn't."

15

"Can I come in?" Beverly Thomas asked, peering into Spur's hotel room.

"It's gone!" Spur thundered.

"What's gone?"

"I left it here an hour ago—less than an hour!" Spur yelled. "Of all the stupid things . . . ."

Beverly glanced around the room. "My god! You've been robbed!" She pressed her hand to her mouth.

"Yeah, and the saddle's missing." Had Amory stolen it? Not likely. He didn't know where the dies had been hidden. Noticing something that had been pushed under the bed, Spur pulled out a dirty, torn prison uniform.

"You mean the saddle that you—"

Spur nodded, rose and flipped her his key. "Lock the place up. I'll be back—sometime." He strode to the door.

"What's that supposed to mean?" Beverly asked, fumbling with the slender iron key.

"I'll be back when I find that saddle and not before!"

The air outside was still warm from the heat of the day. Two carriages rushed by, kicking up clouds of dust. Spur pumped his arms as he headed for Sheriff Tate's office. As he arrived there he saw four men tying their mounts to the rail before it. Dim light spilling out from the windows of the sheriff's office lit the men up.

"Where's Tate?" Spur asked the first man he saw, a tall, gangly youth with bright red hair sticking out beneath his hat.

"He'll be here any minute. We wuz just out catching a runaway prisoner. Seems he broke into the hotel and stole someone's clothes."

"And saddle," Spur said darkly. "It was my room he broke into. I was just there and found out."

"I'll be? This's your lucky day. Here he comes," the carrot-topped youth said.

Sheriff Oscar Tate rode slowly up to his office holding a rope. Beside him the prisoner—wearing Spur's clothing—trotted along, gasping for breath. Tate yanked on the rope, forcing the prisoner's bound hands painfully upward.

"Was he on a horse, Tate?" Spur asked as the man handed the leach to the redhead.

"Why the hell do you want to know, McCoy?" Tate asked as he recognized the man, dismounted and brushed off his pants.

"My room was broken into, my saddle and some of my clothes are missing. He's wearing my pants and shirt. See a saddle too?" Spur calmly asked.

Tate laughed harshly. "Hell, if I'd a known that was your saddle I would've thrown it into the bushes. But yeah, he was riding; his mount'll be coming soon."

A man rode up leading a riderless horse. As it neared the office Spur saw the saddle on its back. He sighed in relief—it was his.

"Look, Tate, let's forget about what happened earlier. I don't like it any more than you do.

Lawson Amory could charm the dress off a preacher's wife. It wasn't your fault."

"Damn straight it wasn't my fault!" the hefty man said, huffing. "But I'm glad you got yer damn saddle back. Go ahead and take it and get the hell outa my sight!"

"Well, what about his clothes?" the red-haired youth asked. "Shouldn't we give 'em back to him too?"

"Hell, boy, you want me to strip that prisoner right here and parade him through the streets of Yuma butt-nekkid?"

"That's okay. I don't want them back," Spur said, as he unstrapped the saddle. "Let him keep them."

"I can't blame you," Tate said. "That man smells pretty powerful."

McCoy uncinched and untied and finally pulled the saddle off. The horse seemed to relax as the weight left his broad back. Spur slung the saddle over his right shoulder.

"Go ahead and get your ass outa here!" Tate said. "I got work to do."

"Right." Spur hurried to the hotel, up the steps and banged on his door.

Beverly unlocked and opened it, saw the saddle and smiled. "That was fast," she said. "Thought I'd have to wait up all night."

"I had some help." He tossed his hat onto the floor and the saddle on the bed. It bounced twice before laying still.

"Don't put that thing there, Spur McCoy!" Beverly said.

He looked at her. "Why not?"

Beverly's eyes sparkled. "Not unless you intend to ride me in that saddle!"

* * *

Lawson Amory started his ride west hours before dawn. His horse managed to pick out the trail by thin moonlight and dim starshine.

Okay, Amory thought, as he bounced in the saddle over the uneven ground. So he hadn't had the best luck so far. He was enough of a professional to wait for the best opportunity.

That time at the outhouse behind McCoy's hotel was just a preliminary move, something to get Spur's guard up, to inject the mission with some excitement. Though his ultimate goal was to obtain the dies, he figured he might as well have a little fun with it.

Sure, he could have shot the bastard that night in Little River and, eventually, found the dies, but that would take half the challenge out of the mission.

San Diego looked to be the end of this game— and of Spur McCoy. He kicked his horse's flank, impatient for the next round to begin.

The stage passed through narrow ravines, box canyons and rock-strewn washes. It climbed up a long, treacherous route, rising 5,000 feet from the desert floor. The scenery changed—pine trees and ancient oaks replaced cactus and scrub. Mountains occasionally gave way to emerald-lapped valleys. Streams and lakes glistened far in the distance, reflecting the blue of the overhead skies.

Spur and Beverly rode the stage for three more days before finally entering a deep valley several miles long. Far in the distance, at the mouth of the river beside which they traveled, lay the Pacific Ocean.

Beverly drummed her fingers on Spur's thigh as they sat next to each other in the stage. She'd grown increasingly anxious as they neared their latest destination. The slightest ease in their progress, the quick, regular stops for a change of horses or to eat seemed to rile her. She wanted the trip behind her.

A gleaming white structure topped with several bells sat on the cliffs to the right of them, on the far side of the river. "That's a mission!" Beverly said.

"You're quite right. Almost there now," Spur said, looking at the Christian building.

She squeezed his leg, eliciting a look of abhorrence from the middleaged woman sitting across from Spur and one of delight from her eighteen year-old son.

An hour later the stage halted in San Diego. The town consisted of a wide variety of buildings and houses, from brick monstrosities to ramshackle dwellings. Many were of adobe, constructed in a quaint Latin style, reminders of the area's colorful Spanish Colonial history.

As they crossed the street to a plain-appearing hotel—the Lomita—Beverly gasped. The sun sank low onto the western horizon, charging the water with oranges and reds, spilling multihued light through the clouds above it.

"Honestly, that doesn't look like the ocean we have on the other side of the country," she said, setting down her luggage and taking in the view as a light breeze slapped their faces.

"True. That's a bay."

Beverly looked at the rock arm that jutted out into the color-shot water. "But beyond that point of land out there, that's the ocean."

Spur smiled. "I never argue with a lady—I mean, a woman."

They went into the hotel.

After registering, Spur walked down to the docks and booked passage to San Francisco on a freighter, the only ship that was scheduled to leave in the morning. It wouldn't be luxury accommodations but he figured he could suffer for a while.

Once back at the hotel Beverly laced her fingers with his.

"Feels good, Bev. Well, you going to look up that cousin of yours tomorrow? Trevor?"

She hesitated. "I don't know."

Spur was incredulous. "You've come all this way and you're backing out now? Why?"

Beverly looked away. "I'm not backing out; I'm just putting it off for a while." She paused. "I think I want to see San Francisco."

Spur blew out his breath. "I see."

"So—so I'm going on the boat with you." Beverly set her chin and looked at him quizzically.

He smiled. "Sorry. I only booked one passage— not two."

"I'm sure we'll manage."

"I guess so. As long as you don't mind sailing with tons of hides."

Beverly swallowed. "Hides?"

"Yeah, new leather on its way up to San Francisco. It was the only ship leaving tomorrow."

She thought about it and nodded. "Well, why not? I do want to see the city, after everything you've told me about it these past few days. Why not? It's no skin off my back."

Spur squeezed her hand.

The next morning, Lawson Amory leaned against a Chinese laundry near the docks. He watched as Spur and some woman boarded the FLYING BUCKSKIN.

After the two were well out of sight, he walked up the gangplank and asked if they needed another hand.

The whiskered skipper looked him up and down, nodded his assent and wordlessly directed him on board. Amory hurried onto the ship.

He'd spent a sleepless night in San Diego. The trip had taken longer than he'd planned. Amory hadn't arrived until well after midnight and, at that hour, hadn't been able to find McCoy. So he decided to follow him all the way to San Francisco.

Things weren't working out right, Amory thought, as a deckhand described his duties. Hell, it'd be too risky to try anything on the ship, so he'd keep out of sight until they'd docked.

Then the prize would be his!

16

Beverly leaned against the railing as the heavy freighter steamed into San Francisco Bay. The deck rolled gently on the calm water as they passed several other small boats and various other forms of watercraft.

"Oh, it's glorious!" she said, clasping Spur's waist as a salty breeze pummelled them. "Just look at all the buildings! How many people live here?"

"A lot," Spur answered.

"I just know I'll love San Francisco, Spur! More than I ever could have imagined!"

"I'll like it a helluva lot better once I've made my delivery."

She turned to him and frowned. "Spur McCoy, always thinking about work."

"That's what they pay me for."

He regretted bringing her along but he knew it was far too late for that now. He'd just hope for the best.

The sun was setting behind them, casting a deep orange light onto the glistening water and painting the buildings that studded the twisting, steep hills with the same hue.

Faint glows showed behind hundreds of distant windows as kerosene lamps were turned up. The ship neared the docks, bringing into sharper view dozens of vessels of all sizes and descriptions tied up along the wooden arms that jutted out from the land. Squat, round-sailed Chinese junks competed with fishing boats; a row of U.S. Navy warships sat beside freighters. The bay was a confusion of movement and color as smaller craft tooled around on the water.

A breeze suddenly swept down, kicking up whitecaps on the water and nearly blowing Beverly's bonnet off her head.

She tightened the bow beneath her chin. "It's more beautiful than I'd imagined," Beverly said. "What a big city!"

"Then you're not disappointed you came with me?" Spur asked.

"How could I be? At least I'm still with you. Are you sorry about that?"

Spur paused. "No. Not really. You're taking a big risk but I guess you're used to that. Anyway, my assignment will be over soon."

Beverly turned to him. "I know. And then?"

He looked at her blankly.

"I mean, what will you do after that?"

"Well—"

"I know, you'll be off to who-knows-where." A smile played on her lips. "I know I'll never see you again. But at least I've spent these days with you." She kissed his cheek. "I wouldn't have missed them for the world!"

As Spur gripped her firm, round bottom a tall figure watched them from the prow.

"When are they expecting you?" Beverly asked as they climbed the steep hill that led up from the docks into the heart of the city.

"Either today or tomorrow. I didn't give them

an exact time."

"Well, in that case, do you think we could slow down and rest for a minute?" Beverly panted. "I'm not used to these darned mountains."

"They're hills, and I'd rather I got the dies safely delivered as soon as I can."

Beverly sighed. "Okay. But it just figures—no carriages for rent at the docks."

"And if we didn't have all this luggage we could have rented some horses. No problem. It's isn't far now, not more than two miles or so."

The blonde sighed and turned to him. "How do you know they're still in there? In the saddle? I mean, you haven't looked or anything, have you?"

Spur shook his head. "No. It'd be obvious if someone had torn it apart. Besides, no one's thought to look in there—certainly not that prisoner who stole it."

Beverly shivered in the cool evening air. The sun had sunk into the western sea, enveloping the city in darkness. They moved from one streetlamp to another pausing in the pale pools of light that they cast on the street.

"I'm just glad I wasn't in your room when he broke in. That prisoner, I mean."

They passed a small shop covered with bright red Chinese characters. Inside, a confusion of silk lanterns, tea cups, religious images, kites, robes, strange, small books and lacquerware vied for floorspace. The pungent aroma of incense filtered out from it.

"Let's stop here and look inside," Beverly asked eagerly. "Just for a minute!"

"We've got to go on," Spur said firmly. "As soon as I make this delivery we can stop wherever you want. We'll have dinner in a good restaurant, too. Beverly, you weren't this tired while we were walking in the desert."

She shrugged. "I didn't *let* myself feel this tired there. Here, with all this civilization around us, it doesn't make sense to wear ourselves out."

A carriage slipped past them.

"You wanted to come along."

A man darted from an alley directly in front of them and stood, hands on his hips. His face was dark.

"Hey, doll, you're looking mighty fine tonight!" the man said. His teeth glowed in a smile.

"Can't say the same for you," she retorted.

"Get out of her way," Spur said in a warning voice.

"No."

Beverly walked past him.

"Hey, dump that joker and come on up to my room," he called as they slowly walked away. "I got a bottle of whiskey and a warm bed." The man ran out into the street and stopped in front of them again.

"Leave her alone, pal," Spur said.

"Ignore him, doll. Let's go." His knees wavered as he looked at her, licking his lips.

"I said, leave her alone!" Spur darted forward to the leering man and dropped his carpetbag.

"Get your butt outa here, cowboy! She don't want you; she wants a real man!"

McCoy balled his fist and smashed it into the drunk's stomach. He doubled over, howling in pain, then came up holding a long-bladed knife.

The man waved it in the air. "You want this, huh? You want this to slice open your guts? Huh, cowboy? Show off for the fine looking lady!"

Spur swung the saddle over his shoulder and down onto the man's head. It connected, cracked into the skull and sent the drunkard to the ground.

Beverly gasped as they hurried on. Spur nonchalantly stepped over the downed man. "Beverly, you sure do attract attention," he said, as he picked up his carpetbag and the two hurried down the street.

"Thanks, Spur," Beverly said. Her face was hidden in the darkness; the streetlamps seemed to be farther apart the higher they climbed up the hill.

They finally reached its crest and turned around, breathing heavily. They looked out on the barely visible string of lights that surrounded the bay and at the vast void that lay beyond them.

"Come on," Spur said. "Not far now."

The streets were nearly black. Clouds shot across the sky, cutting off the thin moonlight, blanketing the city in darkness. The saddle cut into Spur's shoulder as they hurried from corner to corner. He roughly knew their destination. The mint shouldn't be more than a few more streets down and two to the left.

The encounter with the drunkard sent McCoy's mind working. Where was Amory? Spur hadn't seen him since he'd deposited the ex-Secret Service agent in Sheriff Tate's jail. He lamely hoped the man had given up but Spur had a feeling that that wasn't the case.

They moved down the inky street, passing warehouses and packing plants that had closed up hours earlier.

Beverly yelped. "Hell!" she said. "I tripped." She poked her boot at a piece of splintered wood.

"You okay?" Spur asked, reaching for the dim form before him.

"I'm fine. Let's just hurry. This dark city gives me the creeps. Where's all the big houses? Where's the fancy restaurants that serve lobster and pate and caviar? Where's the bright lights and fancy carriages and flower boxes?''

"Far from this part of town," Spur said wryly.

He steered Beverly across a rutted, bricked street. They moved laterally from their original direction. Suddenly, in the darkness up ahead, McCoy heard a rustle. The sound of a can scraping along the broken sidewalk.

"What was that?" Beverly asked, freezing.

"I don't know."

Spur cautiously advanced. The darkness was so intense that he could scarcely make out the sidewalk.

He glanced ahead—twin yellow pools of shimmering light swung up toward him, blinked, and then raced off to the left accompanied by the sound of claws.

Spur relaxed. "Just a cat."

A distant meow seemed to echo his comment.

"Spur, I'm exhausted!"

"We're almost there, Beverly. You can make it."

Spur heard a similar sound behind him as they moved through another intersection.

"Another cat?" Beverly asked.

The sound halted, then continued, growing louder, advancing on them.

"I don't think so, Bev."

"Then what is it?" she loudly asked. Her voice was infused with fear.

"Shhhh." They stopped. The sound halted. "Grab my arm and stay close, okay?"

"I can't," Beverly complained. "My hands are full of my luggage."

"Then stay close." Spur's voice was barely a whisper. "There's no telling who's back there. This is a big city, it's dark and we're not walking through the best part of town."

"Okay."

They walked quickly, Spur's boots clicking on the sidewalk. The shuffling behind them continued unabated as they moved.

Damn, Spur thought. Were they being followed? The image of Lawson Amory flashed through his mind. Might as well find out; no sense in taking chances.

He leaned his head toward Beverly. "We're going across the street again."

The man and woman raced across it and continued on down an alley between two three-story buildings. Their boots clattered on the worn cobblestones.

"Quiet!" Spur said.

"Why?"

"Shhh!"

The shuffling approached them again from behind.

"We're being followed," Spur whispered.

"No! How far's the mint?"

The footsteps grew louder.

"Not more than two blocks. It's one street back the way we came."

"We'll make it!" Beverly said.

They ran, shooting down the alley into the comparatively light street beyond it. Spur figured it was better to deliver the dies than to get involved in any more trouble. As they raced along the street Beverly dropped both small suitcases. They banged open as they landed.

"Hell!" she cursed.

"Leave them!" Spur yelled.

"But—"

"Beverly, come on!"

"But all my money and—and—"

Spur gripped his carpetbag with the hand that secured his saddle, grabbed the woman's slender arm and ran.

She stumbled forward but stopped complaining. "I'll pay you back."

One more block, Spur thought, as they crossed another intersection. He dragged the remarkably fit woman down the cross-street, back to their original route, and saw the huge, marble building in the distance. Soft light shone through a few windows, and the steps that led up to the building seemed to glow with an eerie light.

"That's it!" Spur said. "That's the U.S. Mint!"

"Thank God! You're about to pull my arm off!"

A deep, impenetrable fog suddenly fell onto them, effectively drowning the area in silent, wet darkness. McCoy looked down. He could see the lower half of Beverly's arm but that was it. The rest of her was invisible.

Two riders stormed down the street as Spur pushed himself and the girl harder, urging her faster and faster toward the lights that faintly glowed in the distance.

Beverly's arm wrenched from his grip. "Damn!" she said.

"What's wrong?" he asked.

"I—I tripped again." Her voice seemed to be coming from the street. He reached down with one hand, shifting the saddle so that it wouldn't fall off. The sound of the footsteps suddenly echoed through the eerie fog.

"Where are you?" Spur whispered.

"I'm—" Beverly's words were cut off.

A low, ominous rumble shook through the area.

"Beverly, where are you?" he repeated.

Silence. The fog deposited thick droplets of water on his face and hat as he stood desperately searching for the blonde woman.

"Looking for something?" a voice called out

from behind him.

Lawson! Spur thought. He spun around but the fog completely concealed the speaker.

"Beverly!"

"I'm afraid she can't answer you now, Mr. McCoy. Why don't you give me what I want? You can have the girl back."

Spur walked toward the voice. The fog was confusing; he couldn't see three feet in front of him.

Then it cleared—as quickly as it had descended the fog swirled up into the sky, accompanied by a strong, salt-laden breeze.

Lawson Amory stood ten feet away. He clutched Beverly Thomas to his chest, a gun pointed at her throat.

"No more time for talk, McCoy!" Lawson said bitterly. "Give me the dies or I'll kill her!"

17

The thick, wet fog swirled down around Spur,
Beverly and the man who held the gun to her neck,
temporarily cutting them off from each other's
view.

"Do it now, McCoy!" Lawson Amory said.
"Throw your gun into the street, lay the saddle
down beside it, then turn around and walk away.
You'll get the girl—unharmed."

Spur laughed. "What makes you so interested in
my saddle?" he asked, peering through the
shifting, dense cloud that enveloped them.

"Don't give me that, asshole! That's the only
place you could've hidden the dies. I've got to hand
it to you; that was pretty smart."

Beverly squealed in the darkness. Spur stepped
forward three feet. The fog suddenly lifted,
revealing the pair again. Beverly cringed at the
man's touch but was completely immobilized.

"You're crazy, Amory. You think you're so
smart. What makes you think I've got the dies?
Hear some story from another agent? Hell, use
your brain. I'm one of the fake couriers that
General Halleck sent out to put bastards like you
off the trail of the real one. Sorry, I don't have
them. The courier with the real dies won't leave

Denver for two weeks. You've failed your last mission, Amory.''

Lawson pulled Beverly's head back, gripped her mouth and jabbed the barrel under her chin. She gave out a muffled yelp. "Good try. Now do what I say or I'll kill you both!"

Spur snorted. "Hell, Amory, I always heard you were one of the brightest agents. I can't believe you fell for that stupid story. Who'd you hear it from? Did you get one of the other couriers drunk?''

"I've followed you from Denver," he said, his voice rising. "I've tracked you every step of the way. You've got them and you're gonna give them to me!" He ran the barrel back and forth on Beverly's throat. "Or do you wanna see this pretty little lady die?''

"She ain't no lady," Spur said. "But if you're so interested in my saddle—here, take it." Spur swung it off his shoulder and threw it as hard as he could. It skidded to the cobblestones ten feet from Lawson.

"Your weapon too, damnit!" the man yelled.

"Sorry. I don't give that up too easy. You have to take it from me.''

"I'll kill—"

"Cut the crap, Amory!" Spur said, snarling. "You know you won't hurt her. You're not the kind. Where's the excitement, the danger? Killing an unarmed, defenseless woman's about as tough as shooting fish!''

A low rumble shot through the area. The ground shook. Buildings swayed in the night air. Somewhere in the distance a window fell, breaking the silence as it shattered on the street far below.

"Let her go, Amory. If you want the dies let's do this man to man. You really need to threaten a woman to get them from me?" Spur put his hands on his hips, daring the man. "You really need to hide behind a girl? That's not your reputation. That's not your style. I thought you had some guts, Lawson. Am I wrong? Hell, I don't think you quit the service. I think they kicked you out cause you're scared."

"Bastard!" Amory said.

The earth moved and shook. Lawson looked around him wildly. "What—what the hell's happening?"

"It's just an earthquake. Christ; even that scares you!" Spur laughed raucously and cracked his knuckles. "You don't need her. Let her go, Amory!"

"Say goodbye to your piece of ass, McCoy! I'm tired of all your jabbering!"

He cocked the .45 Beverly closed her eyes. Amory started to pull the trigger.

The ground split open a dozen yards from them, swallowing an entire one-story building. The earthquake nearly knocked Spur's feet out from under him. He staggered, his eyes riveted on the ex-Secret Service agent, waiting for his chance.

Tons of shaking earth produced a cacaphony of destruction. Windows shattered. Thousands of bricks splattered onto the street around them.

"Let her go!" Spur said, regaining his balance.

"What the hell, take her!"

Lawson Amory thrust the woman toward him and darted for the saddle that lay in the middle of the street. Spur drew his long-barrelled .45. The wall ten feet in front of him buckled and started to collapse. Spur darted forward, grabbed Beverly and yanked her to safety. They slammed onto the ground as dust and debris rained down on the sidewalk, just missing them.

Beverly sobbed, hiding her eyes as the tremor continued to shake through the city.

The dust diffused the scene. Spur coughed and choked on the vile wall-particles as he stood on the shaky ground. He wiped stinging grit from his eyes as he struggled to fix his aim on the man who bent down to retrieve his saddle.

He had the Colt lined up, ready to fire. The quake increased in force, roaring directly underneath them. The street seemed to liquify, rippling and shifting as the earth shook and tossed both men onto its surface.

"Goddamnit!" Spur shouted, picking himself up from the ground as Amory rose to his feet again. His left leg ached.

"Don't do it, Amory!"

The man hoisted the saddle.

"Is it worth it?"

The man's answer was lost in an ear-splitting crush. Four windows fell, splashing the ground between the two men with thousands of razor-sharp fragments.

Amory turned to run, still gripping the saddle. Spur fired as the street boiled beneath him again. The shot went wild, slamming into a large pane of glass.

"Damn!"

Lawson Amory laughed as he ran through the darkened street. "Can't shoot better than that, Spur?"

Furious, McCoy darted toward the departing figure. His boots crushed the glass to dust as he moved over the slippery, hazardous terrain. His ears ached with the earth's roar.

Amory rounded a corner up ahead.

Spur reached it and halted. He breathed heavily

as the tremor rattled through the city and slowly died off.

The silence was eerie. McCoy pressed his back against the warehouse's wall, waiting. No sounds of footsteps. Amory must be standing just around the corner, waiting for him to step out.

"McCoy! You want the dies? Come and get them!"

The voice was near—too near. Spur glanced down at the street, bent and hoisted a two-foot-long piece of wood that had been wrenched from the building by the quake. He threw it past the corner.

Two shots pierced the night.

"Nice try, McCoy!" Lawson said.

Spur heard Beverly's sobs far away. He silenced his breath, poured all his concentration into his right hand, into the finger that gently gripped the cold metal trigger.

He had to move fast. He wouldn't have a second chance, no time to correct his aim.

Spur spun around the corner and fired.

Amory screamed as the slug slammed into his left arm. The agent's .45 spoke, spitting hot lead as Spur darted back around the corner.

He heard the heavy sound of leather slapping the street as Lawson dropped the saddle.

"Give it up, Amory!"

"No fuckin' way! I've worked too long to let some bastard like you—"

Another spin, another shot. The bullet slammed into Amory's right arm, ripping the muscles apart, severing veins and arteries.

He ducked back around the corner as Lawson screamed and fired four slugs at Spur.

"I won't kill you," McCoy shouted. "Unless you

force me to. You know the rules." He emerged from the corner and faced the man.

"Shit!" the agent said, pulling on empty chambers. He threw the harmless weapon at Spur.

McCoy ducked and it rattled beside him. Amory crumpled to the street, beside the saddle, and pressed his head to his knees.

"Come on, Amory. Get up. Time we got those wounds looked at." Spur approached the man cautiously.

"Damnit. Damnit! *Damnit!*" The big man howled like a wounded deer. Blood soaked his shirt from the open holes through his arms.

"Amory, let's go." He walked to within five feet of the downed man.

"Never!" The man bent upward, screamed and hurled a ten-inch piece of glass straight at McCoy's stomach.

Spur fired automatically. The bullet shattered the glass and continued on its path, slamming deep inside the man's chest. Lawson choked, coughed, his eyes wild with pain and surprise.

He fell onto his back, panting, wincing as white-hot pain shook through him. "Damn!" The word was harsh.

Spur watched him die. Lawson Amory, ex-Secret Service agent, squeezed his eyes shut. A shudder travelled through him. His breath grew faint; the pounding in his chest ceased.

The man's body fell limp. His face relaxed, the muscles easing into limpness, never to contract again.

The death-rattle shook the big man. A long, lingering stream of air hissed out between Amory's lips like a hot summer breeze.

Lawson Amory was dead.

Spur checked his neck to confirm it, shook his

head and picked up the saddle.

Beverly Thomas ran up, wiping tears from her face. She stopped as she saw the man lying on the street.

"Spur, I—I—"

"I know."

Bev went to him. She stared into his eyes and held out her arms. "Hold me!"

"I will, as soon as I deliver this damn thing to the mint. You understand?"

She nodded, wrapped her arm around him and walked away from the scene.

In an office on the top floor of the San Francisco Mint, a black-suited man sliced through the leather, snipping away the seams that the Denver saddlemaker had so expertly resewn.

Beverly stood next to Spur in the darkened office. The man worked in a pool of light cast by twin kerosene lamps in his walnut-panelled office.

"It should be right there," Spur said as the official peeled back a layer of leather.

"There it is." Mason Galde pointed to the small cloth-wrapped box that had been inserted into a hole dug into the layers of leather. He removed it from its hiding place and set it on the desk. Coughing, he relit his cigar, removed the cloth and opened the metal box.

Inside, gleaming in the soft light, were two small metallic objects, each a perfect negative impression of one face of the American double-eagle, the $20 gold coin.

Spur looked down at it and shook his head. How many men had died trying to steal the harmless pieces of metal? How many lives had been destroyed in the vain quest for these small pieces of magic?

Mason Galde puffed on the big stogie and turned over the dies in trembling hands. "They're in perfect condition." He set them down. "I can't tell you how happy I am to see them. You did a fine job, McCoy." He proffered a hand.

Spur shook it.

"I'll be sure to telegraph General Halleck and let him know how much I appreciate this. Any trouble along the way?" Galde asked.

Spur shrugged, glanced at Beverly and turned back to the man. "A bit. Nothing I couldn't handle."

"Glad to have made your acquaintance. You too, Miss Thomas." He took the dies to a safe in his office, worked out the combination and stashed them inside. "We'll put this in the main vault in the morning. Even I don't have the full combination to that. It takes three of us to open it." Galde smiled. "Well, what can I do for you folks? Need a ride to your hotel?"

Spur smiled. "That would be great."

18

A light breeze sent the lacy curtains into motion. Outside the window the San Francisco Bay was a glorious deep blue extravaganza. The city that hugged its waters shimmered in the late morning sunlight.

Spur sat in an embroidered chair, stretching his back. The dies had been safely delivered and everything had been cleared up with the local law regarding Lawson Amory's death. It was time to relax for a couple of days, to regroup, to catch up on his sleep.

A murmur behind him touched off Spur's smile. He turned and looked at the blonde woman who yawned in bed.

"Good morning," he said, scratching his stubbly chin.

Beverly gazed at the naked man sitting in the chair, widened her eyes, then smiled. As she sat up the sheet fell off her body, exposing her perfect, china-white breasts. Beverly Thomas lifted her shoulders and yawned again, heightening her cheekbones. She covered her mouth.

"Sleep well?" Spur asked, rising and walking to her.

She nodded. "Hmmm. For a moment—for just a

167

moment—I didn't know where I was. I thought I
was at home in Boston." Bev's smile broadened.
"Then I saw you and everything came back." She
looked at the rumpled bedclothes beside her, at the
place where he'd slept. Beverly's face darkened.
"It really did happen, didn't it? It wasn't all a bad
dream?"

"No, but you can remember it that way." He sat
beside her and kissed Bev's forehead. "You
hungry? We never did have dinner last night."

She shook her head. "I don't think I'll be able to
eat for a while. Why don't you come back to bed."
Her voice was dreamy but full of promise.

"I'm not sleepy."

"Neither am I."

Spur laughed and rolled on top of her, their
bodies trapping the soft sheet between them. He
held her head, ran his fingers through her golden
hair and drank in her essence as he buried his nose
against Beverly's neck.

"When I think of what I would have missed
staying in Boston," Beverly said.

Spur responded by pressing his crotch against
hers. He ground it—tenderly, gently—against the
naked woman.

"Oh, Spur. You know just what to do." She lifted
his head and, smiling, pressed her teeth around his
lower lip, nibbled and sucked.

McCoy moaned as she chewed and then lashed
her tongue along his lip. He pushed his groin
harder against her as Beverly raised her mouth.
Their tongues met in fiery, liquid passion, darting
together and slashing inside their joined mouths.

Spur slid his tongue along hers, deeper and
deeper, toward the back of her throat. Beverly
moaned and sucked it in. She grasped the man's

shoulders and pulled him closer as they locked together in oral bliss.

His erection pushed against her, rubbing the sheet, heating it up with his passion.

Beverly twisted her mouth from his and gasped. "I can't wait any longer."

Spur nodded, lifted up and ripped the sheet down. He kicked it off her legs.

"Just a minute," Bev said, as she slid out from under him. "I want to give you pleasure too."

Gentle hands on his chest urged him to lie down. Spur relinquished control and settled down on the firm mattress. Beverly gripped him with delicate, warm hands.

"I've told you I'm not a lady; now I'm gonna prove it to you."

Hot breath shot against his penis. Spur trembled as it grew more forceful. He looked up and saw Beverly's opened lips settled over its tip. She exhaled again.

"Beverly!" he said, and groaned.

She snaked out her tongue and touched it to his shaft. The contact sent McCoy out of his mind. He bucked on the bed as she licked and explored, spreading a thin film of saliva all over his rock-hard erection.

"Where the hell'd you learn to do something like —like—oh god!"

Spur shut his eyes as her lips closed around the mushroom-shaped head. Beverly groaned and pushed lower. It slid into her mouth and, after a slight hestitation, pushed down her throat.

McCoy felt his passion rise to new heights. Hot sensations of pleasure shot through his body as she raised and lowered her head, working his erection slowly, accepting him, nourishing herself from his body.

He opened his eyes and gazed at her in wonder as she slurped and sucked. Beverly's lips made a tight seal around his penis as she bobbed up and down, forcing it deeper into her throat with each stroke.

Something within him threatened to explode. Spur gently gripped her head and pulled her off him. He gasped as Beverly looked up at him, passion igniting her aquamarine eyes, her lips slick and glowing.

"Beverly, you may not be a lady but you're one helluva woman!"

She giggled as Spur moved to kneel between her legs. He gripped her ivory thighs, spread them and stuffed his face into her mystery.

"Oh, Spur, I've never—never—"

He chuckled as he sniffed her scent. It exploded in his brain and sped directly to his crotch. Spur lapped at her pink lips, swirled the soft yellow hair aside and plunged his tongue into the tight opening.

Beverly groaned as he worked it in and out, lapping, licking. He lifted his tongue higher and teased the hard button that lay above.

"Spur McCoy, you stop that now!" Beverly warned him.

He sucked and gently teethed, his passion rising tenfold with each salty, unforgettable taste. He buried his face in her crotch and ate.

The woman trembled. Beverly locked her thighs around his head and lifted her lips. He concentrated on her clitoris, pounded it with his tongue, sending her into ecstasy.

"Stop!" she pleaded. "Don't stop!"

He attacked her, slurping savagely. Beverly strangled out a short cry as her body shook and rocked and rolled through an orgasm.

Spur thought he might suffocate between her legs but didn't care. Her passion enflamed him, forced him to give her more pleasure than she'd ever had with any man.

Beverly finally eased off her pleasure and relaxed. She lowered her legs and freed Spur's head.

He looked up at her, grinned and licked again.

"Spur McCoy, the way you treat a woman!" Beverly said, her face slick, eyes dancing.

He pushed up and laid on top of her. His erection slid between her legs and rubbed against the furry patch.

Their gazes locked—Spur's eyes were strained, excited, almost violent, while Beverly's were misty and full of the pleasures of her recent release.

Spur gripped his penis and rubbed it up and down Beverly's opening.

She groaned as the hot flesh parted her lips. "Now, Spur. No more teasing. Just give it to me!" She urged him with her eyes and parted her legs.

McCoy stared at the aroused woman. "What do you want?" he asked.

"I want you to fuck me." Beverly said, as if she was asking him to take her to dinner. "Now. Fuck me, Spur! Make me feel like a woman again!"

He pushed. His penis slid into her, spread her wide, filled her up.

Beverly gasped. "Oh lordy; you're so big!"

"Should I stop?"

She groaned. "Hell no. Deeper, Spur; deeper!"

Another inch. Two more. Spur kissed her again as he slid full-length into her velvety vagina.

The woman below him shook as their bodies fitted together. Spur revelled in the sensuous feeling, in the woman's arousal, in her tightness.

He pulled out to the head. Beverly squealed in

frustration at the emptiness his withdrawal had caused, then sighed as he slammed back into her.

"Fuck me, Spur!"

The brass bed banged against the wall as he pounded into her. Beverly gripped his waist and lifted her hips to meet his.

"Oh yes. Oh god! This is what life's all about! This is it, two people giving each other pleasure. Harder, Spur, do it harder!"

He obliged until he was hammering into her. He raised up and altered the position of his entry just enough to slide against her clitoris. Beverly gasped at the new sensation. Her cheeks shook and her breath was harsh.

She shivered through another orgasm, tightening herself around him. The added pressure was more than Spur could handle. He felt his balls rise in their sack as they slapped against her thighs.

Spur arched his back and screamed as he shot, spurting liquid white fire deep inside her. Again and again he squirted, again and again he thrust, sending himself over the edge and past all rational thought.

The room whirled around them. The bed spun on a cloud of misty sexual bliss as they clutched together, their slick bodies locked in the eternal embrace of woman and man, washed with the warm sweet breeze of the ultimate release.

Spur lay heavily on top of her as reality returned. Beverly groaned. As he opened his eyes she looked up at him, smiling in wonder and appreciation.

"Don't worry," he said. "I won't take it out yet."

Beverly smiled as he gripped her shoulders and rolled onto his side, maintaining their union.

She nuzzled against his chest, licking the salty fluid that clung in crystalline droplets to the hair that grew there. Spur groaned as her tongue flicked and licked and drank.

Finally, after an immeasurable time, he felt himself softening, his passion fading in favor of a deep satisfaction mingled with genuine affection for the blonde woman.

"That was just what I needed," she said, as he pulled out of her. "Just what I needed to forget about last night, forget about all the—"

He nodded. "Me too."

"You're incredible, you know that?" she asked, looking up at him.

He smiled. "Hell, Beverly, I'm just a man and you're just a woman."

She shook her head. "No, it's more than that. Something—something I can't explain."

"Maybe it's what you've been through—what *we've* been through—this past week."

"Maybe." Her aquamarine eyes sparkled. "Hey, Spur, aren't you tired of your line of work yet? I was just thinking—dreaming, really. We could settle down together somewhere. Maybe here, right here in San Francisco."

He smiled. "It's tempting, Beverly, but I can't. I have to do my duty."

She sighed. "I know. I was just dreaming." She reached down and gripped his penis, nursing it back to life with insistent fingers.

"Again?" Spur asked, enjoying the feeling. "You want to go again?"

"Sure." Beverly kissed his right nipple. "If we can't settle down and get married, let's play husband and wife for just one more afternoon. Okay?"

Spur looked at her. He'd have time to send wires to General Halleck in Washington and his office in St. Louis tomorrow. Might as well enjoy himself while he could; he'd have another job soon enough.

Life returned to his shaft. "Okay," he said, grabbing the girl with the aquamarine eyes.

SPUR

The wildest, sexiest and most daring
Adult Western series around.
Join Spur McCoy as he fights for
truth, justice and every woman he can
lay his hands on!

_____2608-2 DOUBLE: GOLD TRAIN TRAMP/RED ROCK
             REDHEAD $3.95 US/$4.95 CAN

_____2597-3 SPUR #25: LARAMIE LOVERS
                                  $2.95 US/$3.95 CAN
_____2575-2 SPUR #24: DODGE CITY DOLL
                                  $2.95 US/$3.95 CAN
_____2519-1 SPUR #23: SAN DIEGO SIRENS
                                  $2.95 US/$3.95 CAN
_____2496-9 SPUR #22: DAKOTA DOXY
                                  $2.50 US/$3.25 CAN
_____2475-6 SPUR #21: TEXAS TART
                                  $2.50 US/$3.25 CAN
_____2453-5 SPUR #20: COLORADO CUTIE
                                  $2.50 US/$3.25 CAN
_____2409-8 SPUR #18: MISSOURI MADAM
                                  $2.50 US/$3.25 CAN

PREACHER'S LAW

In the aftermath of the Civil War, Jeremy Preacher, late of Mosby's Rangers, rode home to find his plantation burned to the ground, his parents slaughtered and his sister brutally raped and murdered. Blood would flow, men would die and Preacher would be avenged—no matter how long it took. Join Preacher's bloody crusade for justice—from 1865 to 1908.